Richard Bamberger

Another Big Story Book

translated by James Thin

illustrated by Emanuela Wallenta

Puffin Books

PUFFIN BOOKS

Published by the Penguin Group
27 Wrights Lane, London W 8 5 T Z, England
Viking Penguin Inc., 40 West 23rd Street, New York, New York 10010, U S A
Penguin Books Australia Ltd, Ringwood, Victoria, Australia
Penguin Books Canada Ltd, 2801 John Street, Markham,
Ontario, Canada L 3 R 1 B 4
Penguin Books (N Z) Ltd, 182–190 Wairau Road, Auckland 10, New Zealand

Penguin Books Ltd, Registered Offices: Harmondsworth, Middlesex, England

Stories from this collection first published in German under the titles *Mein zweites grosses Märchenbuch* (1962) and *Mein drittes grosses Märchenbuch* (1964) by Verlag für Jugend und Volk, Vienna
First published in English in *My Second Big Story Book* (1962) and *My Third Big Story Book* (1967) by Oliver & Boyd Ltd
This selection first published in Puffin Books, 1990
10 9 8 7 6 5 4 3 2 1

Made and printed in Great Britain by
Cox and Wyman Ltd, Reading, Berks.
Filmset in Linotron Trump Medieval by
Rowland Phototypesetting Ltd, Bury St Edmunds, Suffolk

Contents

Rapunzel

For a very long time a man and his wife had wanted a child, but in vain. At last the woman began to hope that God was going to grant her dearest wish.

Now there was a tiny window at the back of their house, from which they could see a splendid garden, full of the rarest flowers and the strangest herbs. But this lovely garden was surrounded by a high wall, and no one dared to go in. It belonged to an old lady who was a powerful witch, and everyone feared her.

One day the woman was standing at her window, looking down into the garden below, and she saw a new bed of the most beautiful green herbs. They looked so fresh and appetizing that she felt a great longing to taste them. As the days went by she longed more and more for the bright green herbs, and when she realized that she would never taste them, she grew pale and wretched and wasted away.

Her husband was frightened and asked, 'What is the matter, dear wife?'

'Alas,' she replied, 'if I do not have some of those lovely green herbs from the garden behind our house, I am sure I shall die!'

The man was in despair, for he loved his wife dearly, and he made up his mind to fetch some herbs, no matter what the cost. When night began to fall he climbed the high wall into the witch's garden, plucked a handful of herbs, and took them to his wife. She was delighted and immediately made them into a salad, which she ate with great appetite.

But she enjoyed them so much that the next day she wanted the herbs more than ever, and she gave her husband no peace until he climbed the wall a second time. No

sooner had he dropped down on the other side than he found himself face to face with the witch.

'How dare you come into my garden and steal my plants,' she said, her eyes flashing in anger. 'I'll see that you pay dearly for this!'

'Alas!' he replied in terror. 'Please forgive me this time. My need was great, for my wife would have died without your herbs.'

'Very well,' said the witch. 'If it is as you say, you may take all the herbs you want, but on one condition: I must have your baby, as soon as it is born. I shall be a good mother to it and take great care of it.'

In his fear the man agreed to everything. When the baby was born the witch appeared immediately, called the child Rapunzel after the name of the herbs the mother had eaten, and took it away with her.

Rapunzel grew into the most beautiful child under the sun. When she was twelve, the witch shut her up at the top of a high tower which lay deep in the forest and had neither door nor stairs, only a tiny window right at the top. Whenever the witch wanted to enter the tower, she would call up from below, 'Rapunzel, Rapunzel, let down your hair!'

Rapunzel had beautiful long hair, as fine as spun gold. When she heard the witch call her, she would unbraid her hair, make it fast round the window latch, and then let it tumble down to the witch, who would climb up to her.

The years passed by, until one day the king's son came riding through the wood near the tower. As he rode he heard the most beautiful singing. He stopped and listened, enchanted. It was Rapunzel, who was whiling away her lonely hours by singing in her sweet, soft voice. The king's son wanted to climb up to her and searched for the door of the tower, but there was none to be found. He rode home, but the singing had so moved his heart that day after day he rode to the wood to listen.

One day, as he stood hidden behind a tree, he saw the witch arrive, and heard her call, 'Rapunzel, Rapunzel, let down your hair!' Rapunzel let down her beautiful long tresses, and the witch climbed up.

'If that is the ladder one must use, then I will try my luck,' murmured the king's son to himself. And the following day at dusk he went to the tower, and called, 'Rapunzel, Rapunzel, let down your hair!' At once the long tresses came rippling down to him, and the king's son began to climb.

At first Rapunzel was frightened when she saw a young man climbing into her room, but the king's son gently explained how her beautiful singing had so entranced him that he could find no peace until he had seen her for himself.

Soon Rapunzel lost her fear, and when the young and handsome king's son asked her to be his wife she thought, 'He will love me better than the old woman.' So she laid her hand in his, and said, 'Yes, I will marry you and go with you gladly, but how am I to climb down the tower? Each time you come here you must bring me a silken cord, and I will make a ladder with it. When it is finished I shall climb down, and you shall take me away on your horse.'

They agreed that he would come every evening until the ladder was ready, for the old woman came by day. The witch knew nothing of what was going on until one day Rapunzel asked her, 'Why are you so much heavier to pull up than the young prince? He is with me in a twinkling.'

'You wicked child!' cried the witch. 'What is this I hear? I thought I had kept you well hidden from the whole world, and yet you have deceived me!'

In her anger she seized Rapunzel's beautiful hair, took her scissors and – snip, snap – cut it off. There on the floor lay the lovely golden tresses. The old witch was so angry and merciless that she carried Rapunzel away to a barren wilderness, and left her there to live in wretchedness and misery.

As dusk was falling that evening, the witch returned from the wilderness to the tower, where she had fastened Rapunzel's long hair to the window latch. When the young prince stood below and called, 'Rapunzel, Rapunzel, let down your hair' – she lowered the hair to him. He climbed up, but when he reached the top he found not his dearest Rapunzel, but the witch, who glared at him with baleful eyes.

'So,' she cried scornfully, 'you have come to find your lady-love! But the cat has taken your sweet little singing-bird from the nest, and is waiting to catch you too! You will never see Rapunzel again. For you she is as good as lost.'

The grief of the king's son was so great that he could not bear it, and in despair he leaped from the window. He escaped with his life, but the thorn bushes in which he landed blinded him. He wandered sightless through the wood, finding only roots and wild berries to eat, lamenting and weeping over the loss of his dear bride.

He roamed the world for some years in great misery, and eventually came to the wilderness where Rapunzel lived. He heard the dear, familiar voice, and hastened towards it. As he approached, Rapunzel recognized him and fell on his neck, weeping. Two of her tears dropped on to his eyelids. At once his eyes became clear and he could see as perfectly as ever.

He took her back to his kingdom, where he was welcomed with great joy, and they lived happily and contentedly for many, many years.

The Wishing-ring

A young farmer, whose work was going badly, sat resting on his plough, wiping the sweat from his brow. All at once an old witch crept up to him and said, 'Why are you wasting time worrying? Just follow your nose for two whole days until you come to a great pine tree that stands on its own, towering above all the other trees of the forest. If you can fell it, your fortune is made.'

The farmer did not need to be told twice, but took his axe and set out. At the end of two days he came to the pine tree and set to work with his axe without delay. As the huge tree came crashing to the ground, a bird's nest with two eggs in it fell out of the topmost branches. The eggs rolled on to the ground and were broken; and out of one egg crawled a baby eagle, while from the other fell a little gold ring. The eagle at once began to grow, until he was half the size of a full-grown man. He flapped his wings, and cried, 'You have set me free. As a reward, you may take the gold ring. It is a wishing-ring. If you turn it on your finger and at the same time make a wish, the wish will immediately be fulfilled. But there is only one wish in the ring. Once it has been made, the ring will lose its power, and be like any ordinary ring. Consider well what you will wish, so that you have no cause for regret.'

With these words the eagle rose into the air, and for some time swooped above the farmer's head; then it shot like an arrow towards the sun, until it disappeared from sight.

The farmer put the ring on his finger, and set off for home. As evening fell he came to a town. There stood a goldsmith with many fine rings for sale. The farmer showed the goldsmith his ring, and asked him how much

it was worth. 'A mere trifle,' said the goldsmith. The farmer laughed, and explained that it was a wishing-ring, worth far more than all the rings the goldsmith had for sale.

Now the goldsmith was a dishonest, cunning fellow. He asked the farmer to spend the night with him as his guest. But as the farmer slept the goldsmith secretly removed the wishing-ring from his finger, replacing it with an ordinary gold ring.

Early next morning the goldsmith could hardly wait to turn the farmer out of the house. He woke him at the crack of dawn, and said, 'You have a long journey ahead of you, my friend. I think you should be on your way.'

As soon as the farmer had left, the goldsmith hurried to his room and closed the shutters so that no one could see him. He bolted the door behind him, turned the ring on his finger, and said, 'I want a million gold sovereigns immediately.'

Hardly had the words left his mouth than it began to rain gold sovereigns – hard, shiny sovereigns, which fell heavily over his head, shoulders, and arms. He cried out with pain and leapt for the door, but before he could reach it to undo the bolts he fell to the floor, cut and bleeding. The shower of sovereigns fell steadily and showed no sign of stopping. The weight of the coins soon broke the floor, and the goldsmith went crashing with his gold into the cellar below. The rain of gold continued until the million sovereigns were complete and the goldsmith lay dead in his cellar, buried beneath a mountain of gold.

Meanwhile the farmer reached home and showed his ring to his wife. 'Now we cannot fail to make our fortune,' he said. 'We must think very carefully how we shall use our wish.'

But his wife knew at once what to wish for. 'What do you think of wishing for more land? We have so little, and the wedge of land that separates our two fields makes life very difficult for us.'

'Certainly it would be well worth having that land,' replied the farmer. 'Perhaps we could earn enough money to buy it, if we worked very hard for a year.' So for a whole year the man and his wife both worked hard in the fields, and the harvest was so good that they earned enough to buy the wedge of land, and still had some money left over. 'This is grand!' exclaimed the man. 'We have our land, and some money to spare, and we have not used up our wish yet.'

Then his wife thought it would be a good idea to wish for a cow and a horse. 'Let's not fritter away our wish like that,' said the farmer, clinking the spare money in his pocket. 'It will not take us long to earn enough to buy a horse and cow.'

Sure enough, in less than a year they had earned enough money to buy a fine strong horse and a beautiful cow.

'How lucky we are,' said the man. 'We have not used our wish, and yet we have everything we want!'

But the woman still wanted him to use the wish, and said to him at last, 'What has happened to you? I hardly know you nowadays. You used to complain at the slightest thing and feel so sorry for yourself. But now, when you can wish for the whole world, you work and slave and seem quite contented with your lot. You could be a king if you wanted, or the wealthiest farmer in the whole world, with coffers full of gold – yet you cannot make up your mind what to choose.'

'Stop pestering and nagging,' said the farmer. 'We are both still young and we have all our life before us. The ring has only one wish, and that will be quickly used up. Who knows when we shall be in difficulties and shall want to use the ring? Do we need anything? Haven't we been so successful since we have had the ring that we are the envy of all our neighbours? In the meantime, be content with thinking what to wish for.'

With that the matter was at an end for the time being, and it really seemed as if the ring had brought luck to the house and the farm, for the barns and store-rooms were full to overflowing. Year followed year, and the poor, thin farmer became a rich, fat farmer, who worked hard in the fields with his men as if he meant to earn the whole world. But on summer evenings he sat at his front door, comfortable and contented with life, nodding a good evening to all who passed.

So the years went by. Now and then, when they were alone and there was no one near by to hear, the woman would remind her husband of the ring and make all kinds of suggestions for wishes. But the farmer would reply that they still had time. And so his wife reminded him less and less often, until the ring was scarcely ever mentioned. From time to time the farmer would still twiddle the ring

15

on his finger and look at it, but he was always very careful not to make a wish.

After thirty or forty years the farmer and his wife had grown old and their hair was snowy-white, and they had still not used up their wish. And then, both on the same night, they died peacefully in their sleep.

At the funeral their children and their children's children stood sadly round the two coffins. One of them wanted to take off his father's ring, but the eldest son said, 'No, let Father take his ring into the grave with him. When he was alive he had his own little mystery about it, and I often caught Mother looking at it. It must be a keepsake – Mother probably gave it to him when they were young.'

So the ring was buried with the old farmer – a wishing-ring which was not really a wishing-ring, but which had nevertheless brought as much good fortune to the house as any man could have wished for. For a poor thing in the hands of a good man is always worth much more than a good thing in the hands of a bad man.

Simeli Hill

There were once two brothers, of whom one was rich and the other poor. The rich brother gave nothing to his poor brother, who often could not afford to buy bread for his wife and children.

One day the poor brother was pushing his hand-cart through the woods, when he came upon a rocky hillock which he had never seen before. He gazed at it, open-mouthed, but not for long. Twelve wild-looking men came marching through the woods. He thought they must be robbers, so he quickly hid his cart and climbed a tree, where he waited to see what would happen.

The twelve men went straight past his tree and stopped

16

at the foot of the hillock. 'Semsi Hill, Semsi Hill, open up!' they cried.

A wide split appeared in the rocky hillock, and the twelve men trooped in, the split closing up behind them. After a while it opened again and the men came out with heavy sacks on their shoulders. The last man out turned and said, 'Semsi Hill, Semsi Hill, close up!' – and the split closed, leaving no sign to show where it had been.

When the twelve men were out of sight, the poor man climbed down from his tree, curious to know what was hidden in the hillock. 'Semsi Hill, Semsi Hill, open up!' he said. The hillside opened, and in he went. He found himself in a vast cave full of gold and silver, and countless heaps of pearls and glittering jewels.

The poor fellow stood gazing in amazement at the treasure, wondering whether he should take anything. At last he filled his pockets with gold, but he did not touch the pearls or the precious stones. When he came out of the hillock he turned and said, 'Semsi Hill, Semsi Hill, close up!' The split in the hillside closed, and the poor man returned home.

Now all his troubles were over. He lived well and happily, gave generously to the poor and did good to everybody. When the money came to an end, however, he went to his rich brother and borrowed a bucket, which he used to fetch more gold from the hillock; but still he left the jewels untouched. When the time came for a third visit, he again borrowed his brother's bucket. But the rich brother had been jealous for a long time and could not understand where all this wealth was coming from – nor what his brother wanted with his bucket. He was a cunning fellow, and he poured tar into the bottom of the bucket. When the bucket was returned to him he found a gold coin stuck in the tar, so he went to his brother and asked, 'What have you been measuring in my bucket?'

'Corn and barley,' came the reply.

Then the rich brother showed him the gold piece in the tar, and threatened to bring him to trial if he did not tell the truth. So the poor brother told him all about Semsi Hill and its treasure.

Without wasting a moment the rich brother took his horse and cart and drove to the hillock. 'Semsi Hill, Semsi Hill, open up!' he cried. The split opened up, and so many treasures lay spread before him that he did not know where to begin. At last he decided on the jewels, and filled his sacks to the brim. But he had been so absorbed in the treasure that he had completely forgotten the name of the hill by the time he wanted to leave. 'Simeli Hill, Simeli

Hill, open up!' he cried. But the hillside remained firmly closed. The rich brother grew frightened, but the more he tried to remember the more confused he became.

In the evening the hillock opened, and the twelve wild-looking men trooped in. They laughed loudly when they saw the intruder, and shouted, 'Caught at last, magpie! This time you shan't escape!'

'It wasn't me,' the rich brother cried in fear. 'It was my brother!' But, though he begged and pleaded, the twelve men would not listen, and he was shut in a dark cavern in the depths of the hill.

The Little Golden Fish

On a sandy beach beside the sea there was once a tiny little tumbledown shack where an old fisherman lived with his wife. They were very poor, and eked out a meagre existence from the few small fishes which the man caught in his net.

One day the fisherman drew his net in from the sea, but it was so much heavier than usual that he could hardly drag it up the beach. When he looked to see what he had caught, however, there was nothing in the net apart from one tiny fish. But it was no ordinary fish: it was of purest gold.

'Throw me back, dear fisherman,' pleaded the little fish in a human voice. 'Let me swim back into the deep blue sea. I will repay your kindness. I will make all your wishes come true.'

The fisherman was a kind-hearted fellow, so he threw the fish back into the sea, saying, 'You are not worth much to me in any case. Back you go into the sea.'

'What did you catch?' asked his wife when he came in.

'Only one little golden fish – but I threw it back. It pleaded so hard with me, and it even promised to make my wishes come true! I felt sorry for the tiny thing, so I let it go.'

'What a fool you are!' said the woman angrily. 'For the first time in your life you find a treasure in your net – and you let it go! I've no patience with you.' And so the scolding went on from early morning till late at night. The poor fisherman had no peace. 'You might at least have asked the fish for a loaf of bread. We haven't a crumb in the house for supper,' his wife complained bitterly.

At last the old man could stand it no longer. He went down to the shore and called out, 'Little fish, little fish, come here!'

Soon the little golden fish appeared, swishing its tail. 'What do you want, old fellow?' it asked.

'My old wife is angry with me, and has sent me to ask for bread.'

'Go home again,' said the fish. 'You have plenty of bread.'

So he went home, and asked. 'Have we enough bread now, old woman?'

'Oh, we have plenty of bread, but just look at our rain-barrel. It has fallen to pieces. Go back and tell the little fish that we want a new rain-barrel.'

So the old man went to the shore, and called, 'Little fish, little fish, come here!'

The fish came swimming up. 'What do you want, old man?' it asked.

'My old wife has sent me to ask you for a new rain-barrel.'

'All right,' said the fish. 'You shall have a fine new rain-barrel.'

The old man went home, and as soon as he came within sight of his hut he saw a new green rain-barrel beside the door. But his wife was waiting for him, and she sent him straight back to ask the fish for a new hut. 'You cannot expect me to live any longer in this tumbledown old shack!'

Back the fisherman went to the shore, and called, 'Little fish, little fish, come here!'

The fish swam up to him, and asked, 'What do you want, old man?'

'Little fish, please build us a nice new hut. My old wife is always scolding and will not leave me in peace until she has a new hut.'

21

'Do not worry,' said the fish. 'Go home and you will find your new hut.'

Home the fisherman went, and there in place of his old shack was a new hut built of fine oak timbers, beautifully carved and decorated. The old woman came running to meet him, angrier than ever. 'You old idiot, why can't you make use of your good fortune? Do you think a hut is all I want? I'm tired of living like a slave. I want to be a countess with a retinue of servants.'

Once again the old man ran back to the sea and summoned the fish.

'My old wife has become quite unreasonable. She will not be satisfied until she is a countess, with all sorts of servants.'

'Very well,' said the fish. 'Go home, and you will find your wish fulfilled.'

The old man ran home, to find an immense three-storeyed mansion in the place of his hut. Footmen were hurrying to and fro across the courtyard, and the cook was busy in the kitchen, while the fisherman's wife sat in a long velvet gown, giving out her orders. 'How do you like this, dear wife?' asked the old man.

'You stupid lout!' she shouted. 'How dare you call me your wife! Hey, footmen! Take away this dirty old fellow, and give him a good beating!'

Instantly a small army of footmen came running up, and took the poor old fisherman away to the stable, where he was sorely beaten, and given nothing but dry crusts to eat. What a miserable life the old fisherman led! Every day he had to sweep the courtyard, and if he left a single grain of dust lying he was hauled away to the stable and beaten.

So it went on for some time, until the woman became bored with being a countess. She ordered the old man to be brought before her. 'Off you go,' she said, 'and tell the fish I want to be an empress.'

The old man stood by the sea, and called softly, 'Little fish, little fish, come here!'

'What do you want, old man?' asked the fish.

'My old wife is more difficult than ever,' he replied. 'Now she will be satisfied with nothing less than being an empress.'

'Don't worry, old man,' said the fish. 'She shall have what she wants.'

So the fisherman ran off home again. He found that the three-storeyed mansion had been replaced by a towering palace with golden domes, before which all the royal troops were drawn up on a wide green meadow. As the old man stood staring, the old woman, dressed in full imperial regalia and accompanied by her generals and field-marshals, appeared on the balcony to review her troops. The trumpets brayed, the drums rolled, and the soldiers cheered.

Before long, however, the old woman was tired of being an empress, so she ordered her generals and field-marshals to bring the old man before her throne. The order caused great confusion and embarrassment. 'Which old man does Her Majesty mean?' they wondered, as they rushed to and fro, looking for him.

After a long and troublesome search they found the old fisherman hidden away in a corner, and led him before the throne. 'Off you go to your goldfish, old donkey,' she ordered. 'Tell him I am tired of being an empress. I want to be Queen of the Sea, ruler of all the fishes and oceans of the whole world.'

The old man would not go at first, but she threatened to have him beheaded if he refused. So off he went, and called, 'Little fish, little fish, come here!' There was no sign of the fish.

The old man called again – but it still did not come. He called a third time. The sea began to swirl and heave, and the sky grew dark and menacing. At last the little golden fish appeared, 'What do you want, old man?'

'My old wife is quite mad,' he replied. 'She now wants to be Queen of the Sea, ruler of all the fishes and oceans of the whole world.'

Not a word did the golden fish utter, but turned about and disappeared into the depths of the ocean. The old man set off home, and as he came up the beach he could hardly believe his eyes. Gone was the magnificent palace, as though it had never existed. The tumbledown shack stood in its old place, and inside sat the old woman in her ragged grey skirt.

So life went on as before. Once more the old man went fishing; but though he cast his net as industriously as ever he never again caught the little golden fish.

Master Money and Madam Fortune

Once upon a time Master Money and Madam Fortune fell in love with one another. They were always in each other's company. Like the tail behind a dog, Master Money trailed after Madam Fortune, and people began to say that they would soon be married.

Master Money was stout and thickset, with a round head made of gold from Peru, a body of silver from Mexico, and legs of pure copper. Madam Fortune was a chatterbox, moody and capricious, inconstant, and blind as a mole.

Hardly was the wedding over than they began to quarrel. Madam Fortune wanted everything her own way, but that was not at all to the liking of the proud Master Money. As neither would give way to the other, they decided to have a test to see which of them was the more powerful.

'Look,' said the woman to her husband. 'There is a poor ragged fellow sitting at the foot of the olive tree. Let us see which of us can give him the better life.'

Master Money agreed, and out they went to the olive tree. The man was so poor and unfortunate that he had never set eyes on either of them during his whole life. His eyes popped out of his head like two black olives when he caught sight of the distinguished couple approaching him.

'God bless you,' said Master Money.

'And Your Excellency likewise,' replied the poor man.

'Do you not recognize me?'

'No, Your Honour, but here I am at your service,' said the man.

'Have you never set eyes on me before?'

'No, never.'

'Then you have no possessions?'

'Oh yes, sir. I have six children, naked as onions and with rags for shoes. But as for anything else, it has always been a case of "Wait and see".'

'Why are you not working?'

'Because I cannot find a job. I have such bad luck that everything I start goes wrong. A man employed me to dig a well for him here, and promised me a handsome reward if I struck water. But he would pay nothing in advance.'

'Sensible fellow!' exclaimed Master Money. 'But continue.'

'I worked extremely hard, until the sweat was pouring off my back – for I am not as weak as I look.'

'I can well believe that,' said Master Money.

'I dug and dug, deeper and deeper, day after day, but not a drop of water did I find. It seemed as if the centre of the earth had dried up.'

'I will help you, my friend,' said Master Money, handing the poor man a coin. The poor fellow at first thought he was dreaming, but then he took the coin and ran like a

greyhound straight to the baker's to buy bread. However, when he put his hand in his pocket to take out the coin he found nothing but the hole through which the coin had made its escape. In despair he crawled about by the road-side, scrabbling in the dust in the hope of finding his lost coin. But how could he possibly know where to look? With the coin he lost time, and with time he lost his temper, and he began to curse his bad luck.

Madam Fortune nearly split her sides laughing, and Master Money's face became yellower than ever with rage. There was nothing for it but to delve once more into his money-bag and give the poor man more coins.

The poor man was wild with joy, and this time, instead of going to the baker's, he went to the draper's to buy some clothes for his wife and children. But when he handed the coins across the counter the draper declared that they were not real and that the poor man must be a forger, who should be brought to justice. The poor fellow was so ashamed at this that you could have made toast on his burning cheeks.

He turned tail and fled straight back to Master Money. When he related his sad experience Madam Fortune was most amused, but Master Money was furious.

'Take this,' he said, giving the poor fellow a handful of gold. 'You have been most unfortunate, but I will help you if it's the last thing I do.'

Quite beside himself and mad with delight the poor man rushed away, only to run into a pair of thieves, who knocked him down and stripped him, and robbed him of his gold.

'Now it is my turn,' said Madam Fortune, with a supercilious smile at her enraged husband. 'We shall soon see which of us has the greater power.' She went up to the poor man, who had thrown himself on the ground and was tearing his hair. She breathed on him gently, and almost immediately he found under his hand the coin he had lost through the hole in his pocket.

'Oh, well,' he sighed. 'Something is better than nothing. I must buy some bread for my poor children. They have had nothing to eat for three days, and their tummies are as empty as hollow nutshells.'

As he passed by the draper's shop the draper called him and apologized for what he had said. He had thought the coins were false, but the goldsmith had called in and had declared that they were genuine. In fact they were probably worth more than ordinary coins of the same sort. He returned the coins, and to make amends he gave the poor man all the clothes he had previously wanted to buy. The poor man accepted the apology and took the clothes under his arm.

As he was crossing the market-place he met the two

thieves who had robbed him being taken to prison. The judge, who was the most just judge that ever was, gave back the handful of gold coins to the poor man without charging him anything.

The poor man invested his money in a mine which was being sunk by one of his friends, and they had barely dug five feet below the surface when they found first a vein of gold, then a vein of tin, and finally a vein of iron. Before long the poor man was an exceedingly wealthy man, the envy of all who knew him.

From that time on, Madam Fortune had her husband completely in the hollow of her hand. She is more moody and capricious than ever, and distributes her favours without rhyme or reason. It is even possible that she will turn her attention on you some day.

The Little Donkey

There once lived a king and queen who were rich and had everything they wanted, except for a child. The poor queen lamented day and night, saying, 'If only I had a little child!'

At last their wish was fulfilled, but when the baby was born it looked like a baby donkey – not like a human baby at all! The queen was heartbroken when she set eyes on it, and cried, 'I would rather have had no child at all than a donkey! Take it away and throw it into the river!'

'No,' said the king. 'He is God's gift to us, and shall be my son and heir.'

So the little donkey was well cared for, and as the years went by he grew in stature and flaunted a pair of long, straight ears. He was a merry little fellow, always leaping about and playing. His greatest pleasure lay in music, and when he grew older he went to a famous musician and asked, 'Will you teach me to play the lute as well as you?'

'I'm afraid that will be difficult, young sir,' replied the musician. 'Your fingers are hardly suited for playing the lute.'

But the little donkey insisted. He was determined that he would learn to play the lute, and he worked so hard and practised so carefully that he could soon play as well as his teacher.

One day the young prince went for a walk, and came to a spring. He looked in, and saw his donkey reflection in the mirror-clear water. It so upset him that he ran away from home and went out into the wide world.

Over hill and dale travelled the little donkey prince, until he came to a country ruled by an elderly king who had a most lovely daughter. 'I will settle here,' said the little donkey to himself, and he knocked at the palace door, crying, 'Here is a visitor for you. Open up!' The door remained obstinately shut, so he sat down on his haunches, took up his lute and began to play a melody with his front hooves.

The door-keeper stared in astonishment, and then ran to the king. 'There is a little donkey at the door, playing the lute as beautifully as any skilled musician!' he gasped.

'Show this music-maker up to me,' said the king.

When the donkey entered, all the courtiers began to laugh at him. He was offered a place at the servants' table, but he refused it, saying, 'I am no ordinary donkey, I am of royal blood and must sit beside the king.'

With a laugh the king called out, 'Come here, my friend! Tell me, how do you like my daughter, the princess?'

The little donkey turned to look at her, nodded, and said, 'Indeed, I like her very much. She is the most beautiful girl I have ever set eyes on!'

'Very well, then,' said the king. 'You may have a place beside her.'

'I shall be honoured,' said the donkey.

29

The little donkey spent a long time at the court, but at last he said to himself, 'What is the use! I had better go home.'

Hanging his head sadly, he went to take his leave of the king. But the king had grown very fond of him, and could not bear to see him looking so sad. 'What is the matter, little donkey?' he asked. 'Stay here with me, and I will give you whatever you want. Do you need gold?'

'No,' replied the little donkey, shaking his head.

'Would you like half of my kingdom?'

'No.'

Then the king said, 'If only I knew what it is you want! Would you like my daughter?'

'Oh yes,' said the little donkey, 'indeed I should.' He immediately became more cheerful, for that was exactly what he had been longing for.

The wedding was magnificent. After the feast was over, the bride and bridegroom retired to their chamber, but the king had secretly hidden one of his servants there, to make sure that the donkey treated his wife well.

The bridegroom bolted the door, looked around and, seeing no one, assumed that he and his bride were alone together. Suddenly he threw off his donkey-skin, and revealed himself as a handsome young prince.

'Now you see who I really am,' he said. 'I hope you will not feel that I am unworthy of you.'

The bride was filled with joy. She showered him with kisses and loved him with all her heart. But next morning the prince put on his donkey-skin once more.

Soon the king came to their room and called, 'Is the little donkey awake yet?' Then he whispered to his daughter how sorry he was that she had a donkey for a husband instead of a real man.

'Oh no, dear father. I am very happy. I love him as dearly

as if he were the most handsome prince in the whole world.'

The king was puzzled by this, until his servant came and told him what had happened in the royal bedroom.

'Why not hide in the room yourself, Your Majesty?' suggested the servant. 'You will see it with your own eyes, and if you throw the donkey-skin into the fire the prince will have to remain a young man!'

So that night, when the young couple were sound asleep, the king crept into their room. He saw the handsome young prince in bed, and the donkey-skin lying across a chair. He took it away and threw it into the big fire in the hall, and watched it until the last vestige had burnt away into ashes. Then he went back to the bedroom and hid behind the curtains, for he wanted to see what the young prince would do without his donkey-skin.

At first light the prince sprang out of bed and looked for the donkey-skin, but it was nowhere to be found. He turned and tried to run away, but the king was standing in the doorway.

'My son,' said the king, 'where are you going in such a hurry? You must stay with us now that you are a man.'

'Yes, I will stay,' said the prince, 'for you saw me as I really am in spite of my donkey-skin.'

The Golden Goose

There was once a man who had three sons. The youngest one was called Simpleton, and everyone despised or made fun of him.

One day the eldest brother had to go into the forest for wood, and his mother gave him a cake and a bottle of wine for his midday meal.

When he came to the forest he met a little grey man,

31

who greeted him and said, 'I am so hungry and thirsty – please will you give me a little piece of your cake and a sip of your wine?'

'What nonsense is this?' answered the greedy boy. 'If I give away my food and drink I shall have nothing left for myself. Get out of my way!'

He began to chop a big tree with his axe, but the axe glanced off the tree-trunk and cut his arm, and he had to go home to have it bandaged. This was the work of the little grey man.

So the second son went into the forest to fetch the wood, and his mother gave him a cake and a bottle of wine for his midday meal, as she had done before. Once again the little grey man appeared and asked for a little piece of cake and a sip of wine, but the second son was as selfish as the first. 'If I give you any, I shall have less for myself,' he said. 'Go away and don't pester me!'

Punishment was not long in coming to him, for he soon chopped his leg with the axe, and had to be carried home.

'Father,' said Simpleton, 'why don't you let me go and cut the wood?'

'What is the use?' replied his father. 'Both your brothers are skilled wood-cutters, and yet they have come to grief. What do *you* know about wielding an axe?' But Simpleton persisted, until his father said, 'All right, then. I suppose you must learn the hard way!'

As he set out, his mother gave him a crust of stale bread and a bottle of sour beer to take with him. As soon as he came to the wood he met the little grey man, who said, 'Give me a piece of your cake and a drink out of your bottle. I am so hungry and thirsty!'

'I'm afraid I have only stale bread and sour beer,' answered Simpleton. 'If that will suit you, let us eat and drink together.'

But when Simpleton brought out his stale bread it was a

beautiful cake, and the sour beer had turned into the best wine. So they ate and drank together, and when they had finished the old man said, 'You are a kind lad, and willing to share whatever you have. I am going to reward you. Do you see that old tree? Cut it down, and you will find something between its roots.' And with these words the old man departed.

Simpleton rolled up his sleeves and set to work, and in no time the tree crashed to the ground. Between its roots was a goose with feathers of pure gold. He picked it up and took it to the inn where he intended to spend the night.

Now the innkeeper had three daughters, who were full of curiosity about the strange bird and thought they would each like to have one of its golden feathers.

Simpleton left his goose in the stable, and as soon as he had gone the eldest daughter crept in and seized the goose by the wing, but her hand stuck fast and she could not move it.

Soon after this the second daughter came in, also meaning to steal a feather. She fared no better, for she had barely touched her sister when she stuck fast to her.

In due course the youngest sister came in, and the other two cried, 'Take care! Keep away from us!' But the youngest sister thought they wanted to prevent her from taking a golden feather, so she tried to pull her sisters away, and – like them she stuck fast. So all three of them had to spend the night in the stable.

Next morning Simpleton came to the stable, tucked the goose under his arm, and set off. He did not bother his head in the least about the three girls, and they were dragged along behind, unable to let go, tripping and stumbling over one another.

Halfway across a field they met the priest, who was amazed at this strange procession. 'Are you not ashamed, you silly girls, of chasing after a young fellow in this way?'

he cried, and with these words he seized the youngest sister by the hand to pull her away. But the moment he touched her he, too, stuck fast, and had to hurry along behind her.

Not long after this they ran across the sexton, who was surprised to see the priest chasing after three girls. 'Where are you going in such a hurry?' he asked. 'Don't forget that we have a christening this afternoon!' He ran up to pull the priest's sleeve, and immediately stuck fast.

They had not gone far before they met two peasants, returning from work with their hatchets. The priest called out to them to come and free him and the sexton, but scarcely had they laid hands on the sexton's coat than they, too, stuck fast. Now there were seven running along behind Simpleton and his golden goose.

Some time later they came to a city where the king was in despair because his daughter was so sad. Nothing could

34

make her smile. So he issued a proclamation that whoever could make her laugh should marry her.

Simpleton heard the proclamation, and wasted no time in parading his goose and the procession before the princess, who was so amused at this extraordinary sight that she immediately burst out laughing, till it seemed that nothing on earth could stop her. So Simpleton claimed her as his bride.

The king regretted his promise, however, and said, 'First of all you must bring me a man who can drink a whole cellar of wine in one day.'

Simpleton at once thought of the little old man in the forest, and back he went to the spot where he had felled the tree. There he saw a stranger sitting on the stump, with a face as long as a fiddle. 'What's the matter?' asked Simpleton.

'I am so thirsty!' replied the stranger. 'I cannot abide water, and I have already drunk a barrel of wine, but what is the use of such a tiny mouthful?'

'I think I can help you,' said Simpleton. 'Come with me!' And he led him to the king's cellar. The stranger set to, emptying barrel after barrel, and before the day was out he had drunk every drop of wine in that enormous cellar.

Again Simpleton asked for his bride, but once again the king refused to keep his word, irritated by the thought that his daughter should marry a lad whom everyone called Simpleton. 'Bring me first a man who can eat a whole mountain of bread at one sitting.'

Simpleton turned and went back to the forest, followed by his long procession. Here he met another stranger, who was busy tightening a thick belt round his middle. He pulled a long face as he explained, 'I have just eaten a whole ovenful of loaves, but what is the use of such a tiny amount of bread when you are as hungry as I am? If I don't tighten my belt I shall die of starvation.'

'Come with me,' cried Simpleton. 'I think I can help you!' They found that the king had gathered together all the bread in his entire kingdom and piled it up into an enormous mountain. The stranger from the forest set to work, and before dusk he had eaten every crumb of the mountain of loaves.

For the third time Simpleton demanded his bride, but again the king refused, saying, 'Bring me a ship that can sail on both land and water. Then you may marry my daughter.'

Once again Simpleton returned to the forest, where he found his friend, the little grey man with whom he had shared his lunch. 'I have eaten for you and I have drunk for you,' said the little old man, 'and now I will give you the ship that can sail on both land and water, because you were so kind to me.'

So Simpleton sailed back to the king in his wonderful ship, and the king saw that he would have to give in and let Simpleton marry the princess, whether he liked it or not. The young couple lived happily together for many years, and after the old king's death Simpleton inherited the kingdom and became king.

Jack and the Beanstalk

There was once a poor widow who had a son called Jack and a cow called Milky-white. Their only means of livelihood was the milk which the cow gave. Every morning they took the milk to the market and sold it, until, one morning, Milky-white suddenly stopped giving milk. The poor widow thought that the end of the world had come.

'What shall we do now? What shall we do now?' she cried.

'Be brave, Mother,' said Jack. 'I will go and look for work.'

'What is the use?' said the widow. 'You tried that once before, and no one would give you a job. No, we shall have to sell Milky-white and start a shop with the money.'

'All right, Mother,' said Jack. 'Today is market-day, and I should be able to sell Milky-white for a good price.'

So Jack tied a string round the cow's neck and led her off to market. But on the way he met a strange little old man, who said, 'Good morning, Jack!'

'Good morning to you, sir!' replied Jack, wondering how the old man knew his name.

'Where are you going, Jack?' asked the old man.

'I'm going to market to sell the cow.'

'I see,' said the old man. 'But you don't look clever enough to sell cows. I doubt if you can even tell me how many beans make five!'

'Oh yes, I can,' said Jack quickly. 'Two in each hand and one in your mouth.'

'Quite right,' said the old man. 'And here are the beans for you.' With these words he produced a handful of odd-looking beans from his pocket.

'Since you are so clever,' he said, 'I have no objection to doing business with you. Give me the cow, and take the beans.'

'Not so fast, not so fast!' cried Jack.

'Oh, but you don't know what wonderful beans these are,' said the man. 'If you plant them before going to bed, they will have grown right up to the sky by the morning.'

'Is that really true?' asked Jack.

'Of course it is, and if it isn't you can have your cow back again.'

'It's a bargain,' said Jack, stuffing the beans into his pocket, and handing over Milky-white's halter.

So Jack started for home and arrived well before night-fall, for there was not far to go.

His mother was most surprised to see him back so early. 'I see you have not brought Milky-white back,' she said. 'How much did you get for her?'

'You'll never guess, Mother!' he replied.

'Never guess? I shouldn't have thought it would be difficult. Five pounds? Ten? Fifteen? Surely not twenty?'

'I said you would never guess. Here – what do you think of these beans? Aren't they splendid? They are magic! If you plant them at night . . .'

'What!' cried the poor mother. 'Are you really such an idiot? Surely you did not sell our beautiful Milky-white for a handful of odd-looking beans?' And she seized the beans and threw them out of the window. 'Off to bed with you now! Not a bite of supper do you get!'

Sadly Jack climbed the stairs to his little room in the attic, sorry that his mother was so angry, and sorrier still that he had to go to bed without any supper. At last he fell asleep.

When he woke up next morning Jack felt there was something wrong. There was a bright pool of sunlight in one corner of his room, but the rest of it lay in deep shadow. He hopped out of bed and ran to the window, and what do you think he saw? The beans his mother had thrown out of the window had shot up into an enormous beanstalk, which had grown higher and higher until it reached the sky. The little old man had spoken the truth after all.

The beanstalk twined upward just outside Jack's window. He had only to open the windows and take a short step to be out on the beanstalk, which stretched up to the sky like a great ladder. He climbed and he climbed, and he climbed and he climbed, until he reached the sky. When he stepped into the sky he found himself on a long wide road which led, straight as an arrow, into the distance. Jack followed the road until he came to a big, big house, in the doorway of which stood a big, big woman.

'Good morning, good lady,' said Jack as politely as he could. 'Could you possibly let me have something for breakfast?' You will remember that Jack had been sent to bed without any supper, and by this time he was ravenous.

'You want breakfast, do you?' said the woman. 'You'll be the breakfast yourself if you don't run away quickly. My husband is a giant, and his favourite dish is roast boy on toast. He will be here immediately.'

'Please, dear lady,' begged Jack, 'give me just a morsel to eat. I have had nothing to eat since yesterday morning, and it's all the same to me whether I am roasted or starved to death.'

The giant's wife was not as bad as she seemed, for she took Jack into the kitchen and gave him a thick piece of bread and cheese and a mug of milk. But hardly had Jack begun to eat than – thud! thud! thud! – the whole house began to shake with the footsteps of the approaching giant.

'For heaven's sake, here's my husband!' cried the giant's wife. 'What can I do? Quickly, jump in here!' And she pushed Jack into the oven just as the giant came into the room.

He was an enormous giant, bigger than any you have ever seen, and he had three calves roped to his belt. He untied a couple and threw them on to the kitchen table, saying, 'There you are, my dear. Roast me a couple for breakfast!' He sat down to wait for his meal to be cooked, but almost immediately he sniffed the air, jumped to his feet, and roared, 'What do I smell? Human flesh?'

'Nonsense, my dear,' said his wife. 'You must be dreaming – unless you can smell the remains of the tasty little boy you had for breakfast yesterday. Go and wash your hands, and your breakfast will be ready as soon as you come back.'

As soon as he had gone Jack tried to jump out of the oven and run away, but the woman said, 'Wait till he's asleep. He always take a nap after his breakfast.'

The giant ate his two calves for breakfast; then he went to a huge chest by the wall and took out a bag of money, which he started to count. As he counted, his head began to nod until he was fast asleep, sprawled across the table. The whole house shook with his snoring.

On tiptoe Jack crept out of the oven, tucked the bag of money under his arm as he passed the giant, and ran to the top of the beanstalk as fast as his legs would carry him. He threw the sack of money into his mother's garden, and then he climbed down the beanstalk and in at his bedroom window. He told his mother all that had happened, showed her the bag of money, and said, 'Well, Mother dear, was I not right about the beans? How do you like their magic now?'

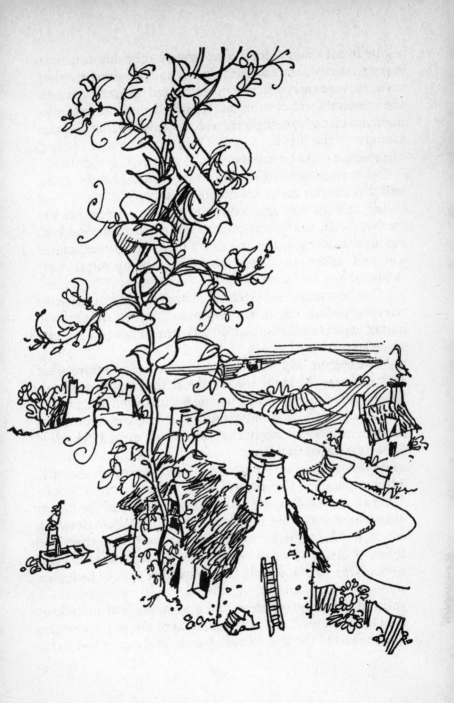

The money lasted for a long time, but in due course it was exhausted, and Jack decided to pay the giant another visit. He rose early one fine morning and stepped out on to the beanstalk. He climbed and climbed and climbed until he found himself on the long wide road, which he followed straight to the big, big house. Once again he met the big, big woman on the doorstep.

'Good morning, good lady,' said Jack as boldly as he could. 'Can you give me a bite of breakfast?'

'Be off with you, quickly,' said the fat woman, 'or my husband will make mincemeat of you for *his* breakfast. Besides, aren't you the rascal who was here once before? Do you know anything about the bag of money my husband lost that day?'

'That's strange,' said Jack. 'Perhaps I could tell you how that happened, but at the moment I am so desperately hungry that I cannot possibly talk until I have had something to eat.'

Now the big, big woman was so curious to know what Jack had to say that she took him into the kitchen and gave him some food. But hardly had he begun his breakfast than he heard – thud! thud! thud! – the giant's footsteps approaching. Once again the giant's wife quickly bundled Jack into the oven to hide.

As he had done before, the giant stamped into the kitchen, sniffed the air and said, 'What is this I smell? Human flesh?' But his wife calmed him and gave him three roast oxen for breakfast. When he had finished, he ordered his wife to bring him his hen that laid golden eggs. So the woman brought the hen, and the giant said, 'Lay!' Immediately the hen laid one egg of pure gold.

Soon the giant began to nod and snore, and the whole house shook with the noise. Jack crept out of the oven on tiptoe, seized the hen in both hands, and ran as fast as his legs would carry him. But the hen began to cackle, and the giant woke just as Jack ran out of the front door. 'Woman, woman, what have you done with my hen?' shouted the giant to his wife. 'What do you mean, my dear?' asked his wife. And that was all Jack heard, for he raced off to the beanstalk and slid quickly down it, as if he were being pursued by a dozen devils. He showed his mother the wonderful hen, and said, 'Lay!' And immediately the hen laid a golden egg.

But Jack was not satisfied. Before long he decided to try his luck with the beanstalk again. One fine morning he rose early, stepped out on to the beanstalk, and climbed and climbed and climbed until he reached the sky for a third time. He was more careful than he had been on his two other visits. Instead of going straight up the road he hid in a bush until he saw the giant's wife going to the well with a bucket. Quick as a flash, he slipped into the house and hid inside an enormous copper pan in the kitchen. Not long afterwards the house shook with the – thud! thud! thud! – of the giant coming into the kitchen with his wife. Jack cowered down inside the pan.

'What is this I smell? Human flesh?' said the giant, sniffing the air. And his wife replied, 'It must be that rascally boy who stole your money-bag and your hen. He will be hiding in the oven.'

They both rushed to the oven door, but fortunately for Jack he was not there. 'You and your "I smell human flesh!"' cried the giant's wife. 'It must be the little boy I cooked for your breakfast. After all these years you ought to be able to tell the difference between live boy and cooked boy!'

So the giant sat down to his breakfast. After a few minutes, however, he leapt to his feet, muttering, 'I could have sworn . . .' And he rummaged through the cupboard and all the drawers in the sideboard, one after the other. He looked everywhere he could think of – but luckily not inside the copper pan.

When his breakfast was finished, the giant called for his golden harp, which his wife brought and placed on the table before him. 'Sing!' he ordered, and the harp at once began to sing beautifully, and went on singing till the giant was fast asleep, and the whole house shook with his snores.

Very quietly Jack raised the lid of the pan and crept out. He crawled on all fours to the table, seized the golden harp, and fled. But the harp called out, 'Master! Master!' – and the giant jumped up just in time to see Jack disappear through the door.

Jack would very soon have been caught by the giant if he had not dodged him by running in a zig-zag, but when he came to the top of the beanstalk the giant was only ten yards behind him. Jack grasped the beanstalk and slid down it at top speed, leaving the giant wondering where he had vanished to. Suddenly the giant saw the beanstalk at his feet, but he hesitated to entrust his weight to such a slender stalk, and his hesitation gave Jack a good start. But when the golden harp again called out, 'Master! Master!' – the giant flung himself on to the beanstalk, which quivered and swayed under his weight, and began to lower himself downwards. As soon as Jack was near enough he shouted, 'Mother! Mother! Bring the axe, quickly!'

His mother came out of the house just in time to see the giant's legs dangling from the clouds, and she almost fainted away with fright. Jack leapt to the ground and seized the axe, and with one blow he cut halfway through the beanstalk. The giant could not understand why the beanstalk swayed so violently, and looked down to see what was happening. At the next blow of the axe Jack cut the stem right through, and the beanstalk toppled and broke. The giant came crashing headfirst to the ground

44

with such force that he broke his neck, and the beanstalk fell on top of him and buried him.

Jack showed his mother the golden harp, and before long they became very rich from the harp's singing and the hen's golden eggs. Jack married a beautiful princess, and they lived happily ever after.

Myself

In a tiny little cottage in the far north, far far away from village or town, there lived a poor widow and her son, a little boy of six years old.

From their front door they could see the hills in the distance, but round about them lay nothing but moorland, giant boulders and marshy fens. Their nearest neighbours were the wee folk who lived in the mountain glens and the will-o'-the-wisps who played beside the track.

The widow could tell many strange tales of the wee folk who played in the oak trees, and of the strange lights which danced up to the windows on dark nights. But although she was lonely she had no wish to move from the little cottage, for she had no rent to pay. But she did not like staying up late at nights when the fire burned low and no one knew what was going on round about. After supper she would light a bright fire in the hearth, and creep under the bedclothes in case anything strange were to happen.

But the little boy was not at all pleased at having to go to bed so early. When his mother called him to bed, he would stay playing by the hearth, pretending not to hear.

He had always been a difficult child, ever since he had been born. The more his mother insisted on obedience, the less attention he would pay her, and he generally finished by having his own way.

One evening, however, when winter was almost over,

the widow did not want to leave her child playing alone by the fire. The wind was tearing at the door and rattling the window-panes, and she knew well enough that it was on just such a night that the elves and fairies liked to play their pranks. So she tried to persuade the little boy to go to bed.

'It is safest in bed on a night like this,' she said. But still he would not do as he was told. She threatened him with the stick, but in vain. She scolded him and coaxed him, but it was no use: he refused to go to bed. At last she lost patience with him, and said, 'Very well, then – I hope the wicked fairies take you away!' He laughed, and said he hoped they would, for he had been wanting someone to play with for a long time.

His poor mother lay down in despair, certain that something dreadful was going to happen. Meantime her thoughtless little boy sat on a stool by the fire. He did not

sit long alone, for suddenly he heard a strange fluttering in the chimney, and a tiny little girl – the neatest, sweetest little thing you can imagine – came floating down the chimney and landed on the hearth. She was only a few inches high, her hair was like spun silver, her eyes as green as grass, and her cheeks pink as June roses.

The little boy looked at her with wide eyes. 'Oh!' he said in astonishment. 'Who are you?'

'Myself,' she replied, in a high-pitched but sweet little voice. 'And who are you?'

'I am myself too,' he replied with caution, and the two began to play with each other.

The tiny creature showed him a great many fine games. She made animals out of ashes, which moved and looked alive, and trees with quivering green leaves beside tiny cottages with tiny men and women, who moved and spoke as soon as she breathed on them.

By this time the fire had died down, and there was only a faint glow in the ashes. So the boy took a stick and poked the embers to make them burn up, and that is how it came about that a red-hot coal leapt out of the fire and landed – where do you think? – right on the fairy child's foot! She set up such a loud crying that the little boy dropped the stick and clasped both hands to his ears. But the cry grew to a shriek, as if all the winds of the world were being forced through a tiny keyhole.

Once again there was a strange fluttering in the chimney, but this time the little boy did not wait to see what it was. He dived headfirst into bed. Slowly his head emerged from beneath the quilt, as he waited, petrified, to see what would happen.

A high-pitched, piercing voice came down the chimney, 'Who is it, and what's the matter?'

'It is I, Myself,' sighed the fairy child. 'My foot is burnt and very sore.'

'Who did it?' asked the angry voice in the chimney. This time it sounded closer, and the little boy, peeping out from under the bedclothes, could see a pale white face in the chimney opening.

'Myself,' replied the fairy girl.

'Well, if you did it yourself, what is all the fuss about?' cried the fairy mother. And she stretched out a long thin arm and seized the little girl by the ear, shook her roughly above the embers, and drew her up the chimney.

For a long time the little boy lay awake, in case the fairy mother should come back for him.

Next evening, to his mother's great surprise, he made no fuss about going to bed when he was told. 'At last he is becoming obedient,' his mother said to herself. But her son was thinking that he certainly would not be let off so lightly if the fairy came to play with him again.

The Dancing Princesses

There was once a king who had twelve daughters, each one more beautiful than the next. They slept together in a room where their beds were arranged in a long line. Every night when they went to bed the king locked the door from the outside, yet every morning their shoes were worn out with dancing, and no one could discover how this could happen.

At length the king proclaimed that whoever could discover where the princesses danced every night would be allowed to marry any one of his daughters he chose, and would become king of the land after his death. But anyone who made the attempt, and failed to solve the problem within three days and three nights, would forfeit his life.

Not long afterwards a prince came forward. He was well received, and in the evening was conducted to a bedroom next to the room where the princesses slept. In this way he thought he would have little difficulty in discovering where they went to dance. The doors of both bedrooms were left open all night, so that he would see if the girls left their room. But the prince's eyelids felt like lead, and he fell fast asleep. Next morning, when he awoke, all the princesses had been out dancing for there were holes in the soles of their shoes. Exactly the same happened on the second and third nights, and the prince had to forfeit his life.

A great many young princes made the attempt, but none succeeded in solving the problem.

One day a poor soldier, who had been wounded and was unable to serve in the army any more, was on his way back from the wars when he met an old woman who asked him where he was going. 'I am not sure,' he said, and added as a joke, 'Perhaps I shall find out where the princesses dance, and then become king!'

'That is not so very difficult,' said the old woman. 'You must be careful not to drink the wine which you will be offered at bedtime, and at night you must pretend to be fast asleep.' Then she handed him a red cloak, saying, 'If you wear this you will be invisible, and so be able to follow the twelve princesses without being seen.'

The soldier decided to try his luck, so he went to the king and announced himself as a suitor for one of his daughters. At bed-time he was taken to his room, and just as he was going to bed the eldest princess brought him a goblet of wine. But he had hidden a sponge in his shirt, and he poured all the wine down his neck into the sponge, without swallowing a single drop. Then he lay down, and soon began to snore as if he were sound asleep.

The twelve princesses heard the snoring and laughed. 'What a pity that these men insist on throwing away their lives like this!' said one of them. Then they got out of bed

49

and in next to no time they had changed into their best dresses, and were preening and primping in front of their mirrors, skipping about in excited anticipation of the dance – all but the youngest princess, who said, 'I don't know why it is, but I feel so strange. I am sure there is trouble in store for us tonight.'

'You are always worrying!' said one of her sisters. 'Don't you remember how many young men have tried to follow us already? Even without the sleeping-draught the soldier would probably have slept till morning.'

When they were all ready, the eldest princess tapped three times on the end of her bed. Immediately it sank into the floor, and the princesses descended through the opening, one after the other, led by the eldest.

Meantime the soldier, who had been watching through his lashes, put on his red cloak and went down through the hole behind the youngest princess. Halfway down he trod on the hem of her dress. She was terrified and cried, 'Who's that? Who is holding my dress?' 'Don't be so simple,' said the eldest sister. 'You must have caught it on a nail.'

When they came to the bottom they found themselves in a magnificent wide avenue bordered by trees with leaves of real silver, which gleamed and shimmered in the moonlight. To prove that he had been there, the soldier broke off a twig to take back with him. There was a loud crack. 'Did you hear that?' cried the youngest princess. 'I tell you, there is something wrong tonight!'

'Nonsense!' said the eldest. 'The princes must be celebrating our arrival with fireworks.'

Soon they came to an avenue bordered by trees with leaves of pure gold, and finally to an avenue where the leaves were of diamonds. In each of the tree-walks the soldier broke off a twig, and each time there was a loud

crack, which made the youngest princess jump with fright. But the eldest princess still insisted that it must be fireworks.

On they went until they came to a lake where twelve little boats were waiting. In each of them sat a handsome prince, waiting to take one of the princesses. The soldier stepped into the boat with the youngest princess, and the prince who was rowing her said, 'I do not know what is the matter tonight. The boat feels much heavier than usual. It is far more difficult to row.'

On the far side of the lake stood a beautiful, bright castle, from which came the sounds of violins and flutes. They rowed to the shore below the castle, and each prince led his princess inside and danced with her.

The dancing went on till three in the morning, when the princesses' shoes were quite worn out. The princes rowed them back across the lake, and this time the soldier sat in the first boat with the eldest princess. On the other shore the sisters took their leave of the princes and promised to return on the following night.

When they reached the stairs the soldier ran on in front, and by the time the tired princesses had climbed slowly up to their room he was lying snoring on his bed. They put their fine clothes away and went to sleep, leaving the worn-out shoes beneath their beds.

Next morning the soldier said nothing, for he wanted to watch the twelve sisters again. He followed them on the second and third nights, and everything happened exactly as on the first occasion – but on the third night he brought back a wine-glass with him as proof.

When it was time to give his answer to the question, the soldier took the wine-glass and the three twigs and went before the king, while the princesses hid behind the door and listened. 'Where have my daughters worn out their shoes?' asked the king. 'They dance each night with twelve princes in an underground castle,' replied the soldier. He described to the king exactly what had happened, and produced his evidence.

The king called for his daughters and asked if the soldier had spoken the truth. They confessed everything, for they saw it was no use denying the story.

'Which of my daughters will you choose for your bride?' asked the king.

'I am no longer young,' replied the soldier. 'Give me the eldest.'

So they were married the same day, and the soldier was promised the kingdom after the king's death. But the princes were put under a spell for as many days as the number of nights they had spent dancing with the twelve beautiful sisters.

The Sorcerer and his Apprentice

A poor woman was once going through a dark wood with her youngest son, Jack. Tears were streaming down her cheeks, for she had many children but lacked the means to feed and educate them all.

Suddenly a man, who had been sitting at the foot of a great oak tree, rose to his feet and asked her why she was crying, so she told him of her troubles. The stranger comforted her and said he was a tailor, and would willingly take young Jack into apprenticeship for three years. But he was lying, for he was not a tailor but a sorcerer. Jack's mother had no means of knowing this, and went off home rejoicing, leaving Jack with the sorcerer, who took him by the hand and led him to a great cave. Here Jack was set to learn the black arts, and before long he was more powerful than his master.

One day towards the end of the third year, Jack escaped

from the sorcerer's cave and hurried to see his mother, who wept tears of joy to see him so big and strong and well. 'In a week, Mother dear,' said Jack, 'my three years will be up and you must come to my master and claim me back. He will show you a flock of doves and ask which of them is your son; for the doves are not really doves, but young boys whom he took into apprenticeship and bewitched. When he scatters peas before the doves, look for the only dove which does not eat, but flutters his wings with joy. That will be your son.'

A week later the mother went to the sorcerer and asked for her son. The old fellow took out a copper trumpet and sounded it in all directions, and at once a vast cloud of doves converged on them. The sorcerer scattered peas before the doves, and told the woman to pick out her son. All the birds seemed to be busy on the ground, pecking at the peas, but one dove alone fluttered about without landing. The woman pointed to this dove, and the sorcerer had to release her son.

Jack was now a highly skilled wizard. 'I know how to make you rich,' he said to his father, who was a poor cobbler, 'but it cannot be done all at once. I will change myself first into a cow, then into a bullock, and then into a sheep. Each time you must take me to the market and sell me. The money will be yours, but I will leave the animal form with the buyer and come back to you in my own form. But you must be very careful never to wish that I were a horse, for if you do I shall be in great danger, and shall lose my power to help you.'

So the cobbler made a great deal of money from the sale of a cow, a bullock, and a sheep. He was able to buy himself a new cottage, and there was no longer any shortage of food in the house. But then he grew greedy, and in spite of Jack's warning he wished his poor son into a horse, and led him to market. The sorcerer was already waiting there to buy the horse, and he paid even more for it than the cobbler asked.

Once again the sorcerer had Jack in his power. He took him to a stable where he chained him up, with nothing to eat or drink, and beat him severely with a whip until the poor horse was black and blue. The sorcerer's servant-lass took pity on him, and went into his stall to feed him. As soon as she unfastened his chain Jack took on his natural form, thanked the girl for helping him, and flew on to the roof in the form of a sparrow, afraid that his master would find him.

The sorcerer, however, recognized Jack in the sparrow and, turning himself into an enormous black crow, he swooped on the poor little bird. Jack flew as fast as he

could, but the crow pursued him closely. At length he fell almost dead with exhaustion into a bush in the king's garden. The furious crow was about to pounce on him when he turned into a little wren. But then the sorcerer changed himself into a sparrow, and so the hunt went on.

At that moment the king's daughter, who was strolling in the garden, saw the struggle between the two birds. 'How dreadful!' she cried out in dismay. 'Why must even the smallest creatures fight?'

By this time Jack was quite exhausted, and could no longer hope to escape from the angry sparrow, so he changed himself into a beautiful ring on the princess's little finger. The sparrow searched for him everywhere, until at last he realized what Jack had done – but still he would not give up the fight.

The princess had returned to her room before she noticed with wonder the strange ring on her finger; but in the same instant Jack changed again, and stood before her in his own form. He explained what had happened, and warned her of the sorcerer, who would undoubtedly come to the palace and ask for the ring. 'If he lays hands on me,' he added, 'all will be lost. The best thing will be for you to throw the ring on the floor as hard as you can if the sorcerer is too persistent.'

Just as he feared, the sorcerer came to the palace next day, disguised as a prince, with many servants. No sooner had the princess been presented to him than he asked to see the ring. In the meantime, however, Jack had won the princess's love, and she would not show the sorcerer her hand. But when he continued to pester her, she slipped the ring from her finger and hurled it violently to the ground. Immediately thousands of peas were rolling about the floor, but there was no ring to be seen.

The sorcerer took out his copper trumpet and blew a strange note in all directions, and a cloud of doves swooped down and began to devour the peas. But the princess had concealed a single pea in the palm of her hand. She hurled it to the ground, and out of the pea fell thousands of tiny black poppy seeds.

Again the sorcerer put his trumpet to his lips and blew a different note, and hundreds of sparrows flew down from all directions. In order to waste no time in pecking up the poppy seeds the sorcerer turned himself into a sparrow.

This was just what Jack had been waiting for. In the twinkling of an eye he turned himself into a great black crow, and bit off the wicked sorcerer's head.

The princess took Jack for her husband, and they celebrated their wedding with a magnificent feast, at which the eating and drinking and dancing went on well into the night.

Foxglove

There was once a poor hunchback who lived in the fertile valley of Acherlow, at the foot of gloomy Galtymore in southern Ireland. The great hump on his back made him look as if his body had moved up on to his shoulders, and the local people were scared of meeting him in a lonely place, although he was quite harmless and the soul of kindness.

His deformity was so great, however, that he hardly looked like a man at all, and some malicious people had spread strange stories about him. He was said to have an extraordinary knowledge of herbs and magic, but the only certain fact was that he was highly skilled at weaving baskets out of straw and reeds, and in this way he earned his livelihood.

People had given him the name of Foxglove, for in his hat he always used to wear a sprig of the red foxglove called

Elf's Cap. His basket-work generally brought him more money than other basket-makers earned, and the envy of one or two of them must have been at the root of all the weird and wonderful stories that were told about him.

Now it happened that Foxglove was on the way home late one night, for his progress was slow on account of the hump on his back, and it was already dark by the time he had to pass the ancient burial mound of Knockgrafton. Worn out and tired he sat down to rest on the edge of the mound, and looked miserably at the silver disc of the rising moon.

All at once a strange, subterranean music reached poor Foxglove's ears, and he thought he had never heard anything so lovely. It was as if many voices were singing together in such perfect harmony that, at times, it seemed almost as if there were only one voice. He could pick out

58

the words clearly enough: 'Da luan, da mort, da luan, da mort, da luan, da mort.' Then there would be a short pause before the same song started up again.

Foxglove listened carefully, scarcely daring to breathe for fear that he should miss any of the singing. It was clear to him that the sound came from inside the mound, and so, when the next pause came in the singing, he took up the melody, using his own words: 'Augus da cadine, augus da cadine.' Then he joined in the chorus of 'Da luan, da mort,' and again sang, 'Augus da cadine,' in the pause that followed.

The tiny singers inside the mound were thrilled at this addition to their song, and decided to fetch this mortal, whose musical gifts so far exceeded their own, to sing with them underground. With the breathless speed of a whirl-wind Foxglove was carried down to them, and he found himself in an underground chamber, into which he came circling as lightly as a straw in the wind. Finally he was set down amongst the musicians, and servants were appointed to bring him whatever he wanted to eat or drink. But when he noticed that the elves were all busily whispering together and glancing at him out of the corners of their eyes, he began to be a little frightened. One of the tiniest elves came up to him, and said:

'Foxglove, Foxglove,
Be of good cheer!
Take off your hump
And lay it down here.'

Scarcely had the little elf finished speaking than Fox-glove felt so light that he could have leapt over the moon, just like the cow in the story of the cat and the fiddle. He was overjoyed to see his hump rolling about on the floor in front of him, and to feel his back as straight and as strong as any young man's in the whole valley. Shyly he looked

59

about him at the sea of elfin faces, and he was so over-whelmed at the warmth and friendliness of his reception that his head began to swim. His dazzled eyes closed and he collapsed into a deep sleep.

It was full daylight when he awoke to find himself lying on the mound in bright sunshine, while the birds sang and the sheep and cows grazed peacefully around him. Thinking it had all been a dream he felt his back, but there was no trace of his hump! Full of pride, he looked at himself. He was dressed from head to foot in fine new clothes! Undoubtedly he had the wee spirits to thank for it all.

He said his prayers and set out for Acherlow, feeling so light on his feet that he gave a little hop and a skip every now and then, as if he had been doing it all his life. No one who met him recognized Foxglove, and he had the greatest difficulty in convincing the people who he really was.

As is always the way, the story of Foxglove's hump spread throughout the whole valley, and soon everyone, rich and poor, was talking of nothing else.

One morning Foxglove was sitting at his front door, feeling very pleased with life, when a wizened old woman approached him. 'Can you show me the way to Acherlow?' she asked.

'There is no need,' he replied. 'This is Acherlow. But, tell me, where have you come from?'

'I have come from Waterford, and I am looking for a man called Foxglove, who had a hump removed from his shoulders by the elves. My friend has a son with an enormous hump on his back, and I thought I might help him to get rid of it if I could only learn something of the magic Foxglove used. Now perhaps you will realize why I have come so far. I want, if I can, to learn magic.'

So Foxglove – who was always eager to help others – told the old woman how he had heard the singing of the elves inside the mound, how he had joined in, how he had been

60

carried underground, and how the elves had taken the hump from his shoulders.

The old woman thanked him a thousand times, and set off for home.

Some days later she came to her poor friend in Waterford, and related the whole story to her, exactly as she had heard it from Foxglove. Then she lifted the little hunchback, who had been mean and malicious all his life, into a cart and set off to the mountains.

It was a long, long way, but what did that matter if he could lose his hump, they thought.

They trudged on for several days along the rough road to Acherlow and the burial mound of Knockgrafton, pushing the rickety cart with its heavy burden before them and pausing only now and then to take a little food and drink or to sleep for an hour. As the two women struggled and panted, the hunchback muttered and grumbled, cursing them for their slowness. His temper had never been sweet, and now it was soured entirely by the discomfort of his hard and bumpy ride.

Why couldn't the two old hags move faster? And why should he have to travel so far in order to be rid of his hump?

On the fifth day at nightfall they reached the mound, and the old woman lifted the hunchback out of the cart, and set him down on the ground.

Jack Madden – for that was the hunchback's name – had not long to wait before he heard the music coming from the mound beneath him, but it was sweeter than ever now, for the elves had added to their song the refrain they had learnt from Foxglove: 'Da luan, da mort, da luan, da mort, da luan, da mort, augus da cadine.'

Jack, whose only thought was to lose his hump as quickly as possible, did not bother to wait for the elves to finish singing, nor did he wait for a suitable pause in the song, but burst in at the top of his voice and quite out of tune: 'Augus dia dardine, augus da hena.' He thought that if Foxglove had been rewarded for one extra phrase he would be doubly rewarded for two.

Scarcely had the words left his lips than he felt himself being lifted up and dragged roughly into the mound. He found himself surrounded by a ring of elves, who were screaming angrily, 'Who has spoilt our song? Who has ruined our melody?' Then one of them stepped forward and said:

> 'Jack Madden, Jack Madden,
> You sing like a crow!
> Where now you have one hump
> A second must grow!'

Twenty of the strongest elves dragged out Foxglove's hump and placed it on top of the miserable Jack Madden's own, and there it stuck fast as if it had been nailed on by a joiner or a blacksmith.

Then the elves kicked him out of the mound, and when his mother and her friend came for him next morning they found him lying half dead on the hillside, with a second hump on his back. For a while they stared at him, and were soon frightened that the elves might give him a third hump out of spite. So they lifted him on to the cart and wheeled him home as quickly as possible. It was a sad sight to see.

Not long after this Jack died, weighed down and exhausted by his two humps, and as he died he cursed anyone who ever heard the singing of the elves again.

Cinderella

A rich man's wife was very ill. As she felt her end approaching, she called her only daughter to her bedside and said, 'Dear child, God will look after you as long as you are good and kind, and I shall always be with you.' With these words she closed her eyes and died.

Each day the girl went and wept at her mother's grave, and she was always good and kind to every living creature. Winter came, covering the grave with a white mantle of snow, and when the spring sunshine lifted it again the girl's father married another wife. The new wife had two daughters of her own, who were beautiful to look at, but cold-hearted and selfish.

So began a time of misery for the poor step-daughter, for they took all her fine clothes away from her, and gave her wooden clogs and a ragged grey skirt. From morning till night she worked about the house, sweeping and dusting, cooking and washing. Her step-sisters played all sorts of spiteful tricks on her, and teased her continually. They would scatter lentils in the ashes of the fire, and would make her sit in the hearth until she had picked them all out again. At night, when she was worn out and exhausted, she was not allowed to sleep in a cosy bed, but had to lie down by the kitchen fire among the ashes and the cinders. And that is how they came to call her Cinderella.

One day her father was setting out to visit a nearby fair, and asked the girls what they would like him to bring them.

'Fine clothes,' replied one of the step-daughters without hesitation. 'Pearls and precious stones,' replied the other.

'And you, Cinderella, what would you like?' he asked.

'Just bring me the first twig that touches your hat on the way back,' she replied.

So he brought fine clothes and pearls and precious stones for the two step-daughters, and for Cinderella he picked up a green hazel twig which had brushed his hat from his head on the way home. On his return he gave his step-daughters their gifts, and to Cinderella he gave the hazel twig.

Cinderella thanked him, and went to her mother's grave, where she planted the twig. As she did so the tears fell from her eyes and watered the ground; and the twig sprouted and grew into a fine tree. Three times a day Cinderella went to weep and pray at the grave. Each time a little white bird would come and perch on the hazel tree, and if she wished for anything, he would throw it down to her.

The time came when the king announced that a ball was to be held at the palace. It would last for three days, and all the young ladies of the land were invited, for the prince was to choose a bride. The two step-sisters were delighted, and called Cinderella to them. 'Come and polish our shoes!' they cried. 'We are going to the ball at the royal palace.'

Cinderella did as she was told, but she was sad because she would have liked to go to the ball. She plucked up courage and asked her step-mother if she could go.

'You?' she said scornfully. 'You are covered with dust and ashes, how can *you* go to the palace?' But Cinderella persisted, and at last her step-mother said, 'I will empty a bag of lentils into the ashes. If you can pick them all out within two hours you may come to the ball.'

Cinderella hurried to the kitchen door and called up to the birds in the trees surrounding the garden, 'Come, all you birds. Come and help me to pick up lentils.'

At once two white pigeons flew down, closely followed

by two turtledoves, and with a great whirring of wings
flocks of birds came fluttering into the kitchen. They
began to peck away at the ashes, nodding their little heads
up and down and dropping the lentils into a bowl, and in
less than an hour they had finished. Cinderella took the
bowl to her step-mother, sure that she would now be
allowed to go to the ball.

'Oh no!' said the step-mother. 'You have neither a dress
nor dancing shoes. Everyone would laugh at you!' But
when Cinderella cried more than ever, she said, 'Very
well. If you can pick *two* bowls of lentils out of the ashes in

less than one hour, you may go to the ball. And that, she thought to herself, will be quite impossible. But as soon as she had gone Cinderella opened the kitchen door, and cried, 'Come, all you birds. Come and help me to pick up lentils.'

Down flew the two white pigeons, followed by the two turtledoves, and with a whirring of wings flocks of birds again came crowding into the kitchen. Peck, peck, peck, they went, dropping the lentils one by one into the two basins, and in less than half an hour the task was finished.

Cinderella was overjoyed, but, when she came with the two bowls of lentils, her step-mother simply repeated that she could not go. 'Do you want to make us a laughing-stock?' she asked, and turning on her heel, off she went to the ball with her two proud daughters.

Cinderella was bitterly disappointed, but instead of vainly weeping she went straight to her mother's grave, and called,

'Shiver and shake, my little tree,
Throw gold and silver over me!'

Immediately the little white bird threw down a beautiful dress of silk, that shimmered now gold, now silver, and a pair of delicate slippers, embroidered with gold and silver threads. She thanked the bird as she put on the dress and slippers, and hurried to the palace.

As Cinderella came into the ballroom, all eyes turned to gaze at her beauty. The prince himself crossed the room to welcome her, and led her into the dancing. All evening he would dance with no one else, and if any other young man came to take her away, he said, 'No, she is my partner.'

They danced until it was very late, and Cinderella was anxious to leave for home. 'I will come with you,' said the prince, for he wanted to find out where his beautiful partner lived. But she slipped away from him in the dark, and hid in the dove-cot in her father's garden. The prince waited until Cinderella's father came home, and told him that the strange girl was hiding in the dove-cot. The father wondered whether it might be Cinderella, and fetched an axe to open up the dove-cot. But there was no one inside, for Cinderella had slipped quietly away to the hazel tree, where she had left her fine dress and slippers with the little white bird.

By the time the prince and her father came into the house, Cinderella, dressed once more in her dirty rags, was lying among the ashes of the kitchen fire.

Next day, when her step-mother and step-sisters set off for the palace, Cinderella went again to the hazel tree and said,

> 'Shiver and shake, my little tree,
> Throw gold and silver over me!'

The bird threw down an even more magnificent dress than before, and everyone at the palace was amazed at Cinderella's beauty.

The prince had waited for her to come, and at once led her into the ballroom, and danced with her alone. If anyone else asked her to dance, he said, 'No, she is my partner.'

When it grew late Cinderella took her leave, and set off for home. The prince tried to follow her, but she slipped away from him and ran into the garden behind her home. As nimbly as a squirrel she climbed up a tall pear tree laden with fine, ripe pears. The prince did not know where to look for her, but soon her father appeared, and the prince said, 'The strange girl has given me the slip. I think she must be hiding in this pear tree.'

Her father wondered whether it might be Cinderella, and fetched an axe to cut down the tree. But there was no one in the branches. When they went into the kitchen they found Cinderella lying among the ashes and the cinders as before. She had jumped down from the pear tree, and had changed back into her old grey skirt, leaving her beautiful clothes with the white bird in the hazel tree.

On the third day, after her step-mother and step-sisters had left for the ball, Cinderella went again to her mother's grave and said to the hazel tree,

'Shiver and shake, my little tree,
Throw gold and silver over me!'

This time the white bird threw over her a dress which was the most beautiful he had yet given her, and slippers of beaten gold. All the guests at the palace were more amazed than ever when they saw her. Once again the prince would dance with no one else, and would not part with her to any other dancer, saying, 'She is my partner.'

When it grew late and Cinderella wanted to go home, the prince went with her, but she ran so fast that he could not keep up with her. This time, however, the prince had been clever. He had painted the palace steps with pitch, and when Cinderella ran down them the slipper from her left foot stuck fast and was left behind. The prince picked it up and examined it. It was neat and dainty, and made of the purest beaten gold. Next morning he went to Cinderella's father, and said, 'I will marry the girl whose foot this golden slipper fits.'

The step-sisters were delighted to hear this, for they both had beautiful feet. The elder sister went into her room to try on the shoe, while her mother stood by. But her big toe would not fit inside, for the shoe was too small. Her mother handed her a knife, saying, 'Cut off your toe! Once you are queen you will no longer need to walk.'

So the girl cut off her big toe and forced her foot into the shoe. In spite of the pain, she smiled brightly and went to the prince, who lifted her on to his horse, and rode away

with her to make her his bride. As they passed by the
grave, however, two white doves, who were sitting in the
hazel tree, called out,

> 'Look around, do!
> There's blood on the shoe!
> The shoe is too tight.
> It cannot be right!'

The prince looked down, and saw blood welling out of
the shoe. So he took the false bride back to the house,

saying that a mistake had been made, and that the other sister should try the shoe.

So the younger sister went into her room to try on the shoe. Her toes fitted in perfectly, but her heel simply would not go in. 'Never mind!' said her mother, handing her the knife. 'Cut off your heel! Once you are queen you will never need to walk.'

So the girl cut a piece from her heel, and forced her foot into the shoe. In spite of the pain, she smiled brightly and went to the prince, who lifted her on to his horse, and rode away with her to make her his bride. As they passed under the hazel tree, however, the two white doves cooed,

> 'Look around, do!
> There's blood on the shoe!
> The shoe is too tight.
> It cannot be right.'

The prince looked down and saw blood trickling from the shoe and staining her white stockings. He took the false bride home again and said, 'I was mistaken. Have you another daughter?'

'No,' said the man. 'Only the scruffy little daughter of my first wife, but she cannot possibly be your bride.' The prince insisted that they should call her, but the step-mother objected, saying, 'Oh no, she is far too dirty to show herself here!' The prince refused to change his mind, and at last Cinderella was called.

She washed her hands and face, and went and curtsied before the prince, who handed her the golden slipper. She drew her dainty little foot out of its heavy wooden clog, and put on the slipper with ease. It was a perfect fit. As she smiled up at him, the prince recognized her as his beautiful dancing-partner. 'This is indeed my bride!' he cried.

The step-sisters and step-mother were pale with rage and envy as the prince lifted Cinderella on to his horse, and rode away with her.

As the couple rode past the hazel tree, the two white doves cooed,

> 'Look around, do!
> No blood on the shoe!
> Her stocking is white.
> The shoe is just right.'

With these words the doves flew down on to Cinderella's shoulders, one perching on the right shoulder, and the other on the left. And there they remained.

On the wedding day the two treacherous step-sisters

were full of flattering words, for they wanted to share in the good fortune. On the way to the ceremony the elder sister walked on the right of the bridal pair, and the younger sister on the left. But the two white doves pecked out one eye from each of them, and on the way back from the church, when the elder sister was on the left and the younger on the right, the white doves pecked out their remaining eyes. In this way they were punished with blindness for the rest of their lives for all their cruelty and unkindness.

Witzenspitzel

There was once a king of Roundabout-Hereabouts. Amongst his many servants he had a page called Witzenspitzel, who was so clever that the king was always showering him with presents. The other pages and servants at the court were all jealous of Witzenspitzel, for, while he was rewarded for his cleverness, they were always being punished for their stupidity.

You can understand, therefore, how angry the servants were with Witzenspitzel, and how they muttered and grumbled day after day, wondering how they could make him lose favour with the king. One of them strewed peas round the throne, in the hope that Witzenspitzel would stumble and smash the glass sceptre when the king handed it to him. Another stuck melon pips on the soles of his shoes in the hope that he would slip and spill the soup over the king's robes. A third servant blew midges through a straw into the king's hair while Witzenspitzel was brushing it. But all their efforts were in vain, for Witzenspitzel saw through their tricks, and obeyed the king's commands without mishap.

When all their plots had miscarried, the servants hit

upon another idea. The king had an enemy who was a constant thorn in the flesh to him. This was the Giant Longjaw, who lived with his wife Fatface in a splendid castle on a crag in the middle of a dense forest. No other creature would live there, apart from Scared-of-hens his lion, Honeybeard his bear, Lamb-chaser his wolf, and Hare-catcher his dog. These were his only servants, and he used them to torment the folk of Roundabout-Hereabouts. He also had a horse in his stable, called Swift-as-the-wind, and on this horse he escaped from anyone who pursued him.

Now there lived next to the kingdom of Roundabout-Hereabouts a very rich widow called Mistress Speedy, who possessed a great many fields and orchards, plantations and farmhouses, and had a daughter called Nimble. The king of Roundabouts-Hereabouts was very eager to join all the neighbouring estates to his kingdom, and he was an ardent suitor for Mistress Speedy's hand. She, however, would take for her husband only a man who could travel extremely fast, so she arranged a race to the church, in which the competitors could use any means of transport they pleased. Whoever arrived first would be rewarded by her hand in marriage, together with all her land.

The king of Roundabout-Hereabouts called all his servants to him, and asked for suggestions. 'How can I be the first at the church and so win Mistress Speedy's hand?'

'That's easy,' replied his servants. 'You must ride to the church on Swift-as-the-wind, Giant Longjaw's horse. No creature can move faster than Swift-as-the-wind. Send Witzenspitzel to fetch him. He will be able to overcome all difficulties.'

But the wicked servants really hoped that Giant Longjaw would kill Witzenspitzel – indeed, they had little doubt that this would be the outcome.

So the king ordered Witzenspitzel to fetch the horse.

The cunning fellow knew all about Giant Longjaw's strange household, so he brought out a wheelbarrow and set a beehive on top of it. Then he fetched a sack, in which he put a hen, a hare, and a lamb, and laid it in the barrow with the beehive. He took a length of string and a large box of snuff, and finally he fixed a strong pair of spurs to his boots, and off he set with his barrow.

Towards evening he reached the top of the crag, and saw the giant's castle through the trees. He waited until it was quite dark and everyone was asleep. Giant Longjaw and Fatface his wife, Scared-of-hens his lion, Honeybeard his bear, Lamb-chaser his wolf and Hare-catcher his dog were

all snoring so loudly that the whole castle shook. Only the horse, Swift-as-the-wind, seemed to be awake, for he was pawing the ground restlessly in his stable.

Quietly, quietly, Witzenspitzel tied his long string between two trees right in front of the castle gates, just a foot above the ground, and laid his box of snuff in the middle of the track. Then he set his beehive at the foot of a tree beside the track, and at last he was ready to untie Swift-as-the-wind. Quickly he leapt on to the horse's back, with the sack containing the hen, the hare, and the lamb slung over his shoulders, and dug his spurs into the horse's sides so that it shot from the stable. But Swift-as-the-wind could speak, and called, 'Longjaw and Fatface! Honeybeard and Scared-of-hens! Lamb-chaser and Hare-catcher! Witzenspitzel is riding me away!'

Longjaw and Fatface awoke with a start when they heard Swift-as-the-wind's cry for help, and immediately wakened Honeybeard the bear, Scared-of-hens the lion, Lamb-chaser the wolf, and Hare-catcher the dog. They all rushed out of the castle together to catch Witzenspitzel, but the giant and his wife tripped over the string across the gate and fell flat on their faces, with their eyes and their noses buried in the big box of snuff. They rubbed their eyes until the tears streamed down their faces, and sneezed again and again, until at last Longjaw managed to sit up and say, 'Bless you, Fatface!'

'Thank you,' she replied. 'And bless you too, Longjaw!'

'Thank you,' said Longjaw, and by the time they had rubbed all the snuff out of their eyes, and sneezed it all out of their noses, Witzenspitzel was far away.

Honeybeard the bear was the next out of the castle gates, but when he reached the beehive he stopped and put his paw inside to see if there was any honey. Out swarmed the bees, and stung him so violently that he fled into the castle, roaring, and slammed the door behind him.

By this time Witzenspitzel had reached the foot of the crag, and he was almost out of the wood when he heard Scared-of-hens the lion close at his heels. Quick as lightning he took the hen out of his sack. It flew to the top of a high tree where it began to cackle noisily. Nothing terrified the lion more than a hen's cackling, so he turned tail and fled back to the castle.

Before long Witzenspitzel heard Lamb-chaser the wolf pounding along behind him, so he took the lamb out of his sack. At once the wolf raced off in pursuit of the lamb, and Witzenspitzel galloped on.

He was already within sight of the city when he heard a loud barking behind him. He looked over his shoulder to see Hare-catcher the dog close on the horse's heels. Quickly he let the hare out of the sack, and Hare-catcher turned to chase it, leaving Witzenspitzel to reach the city in safety, without any further trouble.

The king was full of gratitude to Witzenspitzel for bringing him the horse, but the treacherous servants were furious that he had returned unharmed. Next morning the king won the race on Swift-as-the-wind without the slightest difficulty, and his marriage to Mistress Speedy took place immediately.

While he was taking his queen back to his castle, the servants said to him, 'It must indeed be wonderful to have Giant Longjaw's horse, but would it not be even better to have back all the magnificent robes and other booty which he has stolen from your kingdom during the past few years? That would be a fine gift for your queen! Witzenspitzel is clever – he will bring them back if you order him to do so.'

The king was easily persuaded, and gave Witzenspitzel his orders that very evening. The other servants were delighted, convinced that he would not escape from the giant's clutches a second time.

All that Witzenspitzel took with him this time was a good strong sack and some rope. He reached Longjaw's castle just as night was falling, and sat down on a tree-stump to wait until everyone was asleep. When he thought it was safe he crept forward towards the gate, but hardly had he begun to wriggle through it when he heard Fatface cry, 'My pillow is too low, Longjaw. Fetch me a bundle of straw.'

Quick as a thought Witzenspitzel slipped into the straw, and Longjaw lifted him with the straw and laid him in the bed, under the pillow.

As soon as the giant and his wife were both sound asleep, Witzenspitzel stretched out his hand and gave Giant Longjaw's hair a vicious tug. Then he did the same to Fatface. In a flash they were awake and hitting each other, each of them thinking that it was the other's fault. While they were still fighting Witzenspitzel crept out of the straw and hid behind the bed.

He waited for them to go to sleep again before he crept out. Quietly he bundled together all the finest robes he could find, stuffed them into his sack, and tied it gently but firmly to the tail of Scared-of-hens the lion without waking him. Then he tied Honeybeard the bear, Lamb-chaser the wolf, and Hare-catcher the dog – who were all sound asleep on the floor – to the giant's bed. He opened the door wide, so that a howling draught whistled through the room, and pulled the cover and blankets off the bed. He wrapped himself quickly in the bedcover, and sat on top of the sackful of clothes which he had tied to the tail of the sleeping lion.

It was not long before Fatface awoke and felt the cold wind blowing round her legs. She shook Longjaw by the shoulder, saying, 'Give me back the blankets! I have nothing over me at all!'

Longjaw woke up freezing, and said, 'Nonsense! You

have taken the bedclothes from me!' They began to quarrel, and Witzenspitzel started to laugh loudly. The two giants realized then that something was wrong. 'Stop, thief!' they cried. 'Up, Scared-of-hens! Up, Lamb-chaser! Up, Honeybeard! Up, Hare-catcher!'

The animals all leapt to their feet, and the lion shot through the doorway, pulling Witzenspitzel and the sack of clothes like a carriage behind him. 'Cluck, cluck, chook, chook, chook!' cried Witzenspitzel. This frightened poor Scared-of-hens out of his wits, and he ran faster and faster. When they arrived at the city gates, Witzenspitzel cut the rope round the lion's tail, and the beast ran so violently into the gates that he fell down dead.

Meanwhile the other animals had tried to pursue Witzenspitzel, but they were tied to the bed, which stuck in the doorway, for it was far too big to pass through. They dragged the bed round and round the room, so that Longjaw and Fatface fell out on to the floor. Longjaw was so angry that he struck the poor animals dead in a fit of temper.

The king was delighted at the beautiful robes Witzenspitzel had brought him, for never had anyone seen such magnificent garments. There was a hunting-suit made out of the skins of all the animals in the world, beautifully sewn together. There was another suit made of the feathers of all the birds of the air, and yet another made of the scales of all the fishes of the sea. Fatface's gardening-dress was quite extraordinary, composed of all sorts of flowers and vegetables and fruits. But best of all was the bedcover, which was of the skins of thousands of bats, sewn carefully together and adorned with thousands of precious stones, which sparkled like the stars of the Milky Way.

The king and queen were overjoyed, and rewarded

Witzenspitzel handsomely, but the other servants were furious that he had not been caught and killed by Giant Longjaw.

One day, not long after this, they put it into the king's head that all he lacked was the giant's castle. So the king sent for Witzenspitzel, and said, 'Capture Longjaw's castle for me, and I shall see that you are well rewarded.'

Witzenspitzel was in no way dismayed, and soon he stood once again before the castle gates. The giant was not at home, but he found Fatface busy chopping wood, with the sweat pouring down her face in streams.

'Good day to you!' said Witzenspitzel. 'Why are you doing all this hard work? Do you not have any servants?'

'My husband has gone to invite our cousins to a feast,' replied Fatface. 'But I have to do all the cooking and preparations myself, for my husband killed the bear and the dog and the wolf who used to help us, and the lion has not come back yet.'

'That is hard luck!' said Witzenspitzel. 'But I shall be glad to help you. Off you go to meet your dear husband, and leave me to get on with the work here.'

Fatface accepted this offer gladly, and set out to meet her husband. As soon as she was out of sight Witzenspitzel set to work to dig an enormous deep hole immediately outside the castle gates. When it was deep enough he covered it so carefully with branches and leaves and grass that no one could have guessed there was a hole. Then he lit candles and lamps in all the banqueting-halls of the castle, beat on a huge jelly-pan with the soup-ladle, blew loudly on a long hunting-horn, and cried at the top of his voice, 'Long Live the King of Roundabout-Hereabouts!'

When Longjaw and Fatface drew near the castle they heard the sound of celebrations and saw the bright light streaming from the windows. They were furious, and ran full tilt towards the gates. Crash! – they fell into the hole which Witzenspitzel had dug, and all the shouting in the world could not help them.

Witzenspitzel took the giant's keys to the king, who set out at once for the castle with his wife and Nimble, his step-daughter. Witzenspitzel took them on a tour of the whole castle, and it took them fourteen days to visit every banqueting-hall, bedroom, cellar, kitchen, laundry, scullery, pantry, and attic. When the inspection was completed, the king asked Witzenspitzel to choose his reward. He thought for a moment, and said, 'Give me Nimble as my bride, and Longjaw and Fatface as my housekeepers.'

And so it came about. After a splendid wedding, Witzenspitzel and Nimble lived in the giants' castle, and prospered greatly. But the other servants turned green with envy and, no matter how hard they scrubbed, their faces remained green to the end of their days.

The Flying Trunk

There was once a merchant who was so rich that he could have paved the whole street with gold – and the alleyways too – without noticing the cost. But he did no such thing, for he knew how to look after his money. If he invested a penny, he expected to earn half a crown in return.

The day came, however, when this rich merchant died. All his money was inherited by his only son, who spent all his time amusing himself. He would make paper dragons out of notes and he would use gold coins for skimming on the lake, instead of flat stones. In this way he soon exhausted his great wealth and before long only a few pence remained of his whole inheritance, and all he had left of his magnificent clothes was a threadbare old dressing-gown and a worn-out pair of slippers.

His friends thought it no more than he deserved and

avoided him if they met him in the street. Only one of them felt sorry for him, and gave him an old trunk, telling him to say the words, 'Pack up,' to it. That was very kind of the friend, but the young man had nothing left to pack! So he put himself in the trunk.

It was, however, a magic trunk, and would fly through the air as soon as its lock was pressed. As the young man pressed the lock, the trunk shot like an arrow up the chimney and into the clouds. It flew on and on, but it creaked so alarmingly that the young man was afraid it would fall to pieces.

At last the trunk came down in the land of the Turks. The young man hid the trunk under some leaves in a wood, and walked into the city. No one questioned him, for the Turks wore the same sort of clothes as he was wearing – a dressing-gown and slippers. He met a woman with a little boy, and said, 'Tell me – what is that high tower over there, and why are all the windows so high up?'

'That is where the sultan's daughter lives,' she replied. 'It was foretold that a young man would bring her great unhappiness, so no one is allowed to go near her except the sultan and his wife.'

'Thank you,' said the young man. He went back to the wood where he had hidden his magic trunk, flew in it up to the roof of the princess's tower, and crept through the window into her room.

She looked so lovely as she lay sleeping that he had to kiss her. She awoke with a start, but he explained that he was a god, who had flown through the air specially to see her, and she was very pleased.

He sat down beside her and put his arm round her waist, and began to tell her the most wonderful story about her eyes – how they were like deep lagoons, with all her thoughts swimming about in them like mermaids. Then

82

he told her stories about her lips and her forehead – never had she heard such entrancing stories!

Finally he asked her to marry him, and after a moment's consideration she said she would. 'But you must come again on Saturday,' she said, 'when my parents come to take tea with me. They will be very proud to hear that I am to marry a god! But be ready to tell a good story, for my mother likes a good moral tale, and my father likes a story which will make him laugh.'

'Very well,' he said, 'I will bring you a pretty tale as a wedding gift.' As he was about to depart, the princess gave him a sword studded with gold coins, which were just what he needed!

Off he flew and bought himself a fine new silk dressing-gown, and then he sat down in the wood to compose a suitable story. It had to be ready by Saturday, and that was not easy. By the time he put the finishing touches to it it was Saturday afternoon.

The sultan and his wife and the entire court were there with the princess, and he was graciously received.

'Will you tell us a story?' asked the sultan's wife. 'One that is profound and edifying.'

'Certainly,' replied the young man. 'I shall be glad to.' And this is the story he told. Pay attention!

'There were once some matches, who were very proud of their ancestry. They had come from a great old pine tree in the forest, and they were all a tiny part of this tree. They lay now on a mantelpiece between an old iron pot and a tinder-box and told nostalgic tales of their childhood.

'"Oh yes," they said, "those were wonderful times when we were still part of the green branch. Every morning we had dew-drops for breakfast, and all day long we basked in the sun (except when it was raining), and all the little birds used to come and tell us stories. We knew how well off we were, for the other trees round about had only summer clothes, whereas we wore our lovely green clothes all the year round, summer and winter. The day came, however, when the woodmen came amongst us, and in a single day our whole family was felled. Our main trunk was taken to be the mast of a beautiful new ship that was to sail right round the world; and we, the branches, have the honourable task of providing the world with light and heat."

'"I have quite a different song to sing," said the iron pot, who lay beside the matches. "Ever since I saw the light of day I have been scoured and scrubbed many thousands of times, and I have cooked many thousands of meals. I am the most important piece of furniture in the house, and it is my greatest joy to sit on the shelf, clean and spotless after meals, and chat with my comrades."

'"Let's not waste so much time talking!" exclaimed the tinder-box, striking the steel against its flint to make the sparks fly. "Let's have a jolly evening!"

'"Yes," said the matches. "Let's decide which of us is the most important."

'"Oh no," objected the iron pot. "I don't like talking about myself in that way. Let each of us tell the tale of his life instead. I will begin. I was born on the Danish coast . . ."

'"A superb beginning!" cried all the plates in unison. "Everybody will love this story!"

'"I spent my youth there in a quiet family. The furniture was polished, the floor waxed, and we had fresh curtains every fortnight."

'"What a good story!" exclaimed the broom. "It is quite clear that you know a lot about housekeeping."

'"Yes, that is obvious," said the bucket, giving a little leap that splashed some of its water on to the floor.

'The iron pot continued his story, and the end was as good as the beginning. The plates all clattered with joy, and the broom swept up some parsley from the garden and crowned the iron pot with it, partly because he knew it would annoy the others, and partly because he wanted the pot to crown him on the following day.

'"Now I am going to dance," said the pair of tongs, and began to twirl and kick her legs so high that the old chair burst its seams in surprise. "Can I have a crown too?" pleaded the tongs, panting.

'The teapot was asked to sing, but excused herself on the grounds that she could sing only when she was hot. This was sheer affectation, however, for she preferred to sing only at tea-time in her mistress's drawing-room.

'On the window ledge lay an old pen, which the maid used for writing her messages. She was a very ordinary old pen, and had become badly stained through being dipped

85

too deep into the ink-pot. "Let's not bother about the teapot and her sulky airs!" she declared. "If she won't sing, let her keep quiet. There's a nightingale in the birdcage who can sing the most beautiful melodies, even though she has never been taught."

'"I consider it most unseemly," said the tea-kettle, who was a half-sister to the teapot, "that a strange bird should be given a hearing in this company. I call upon the basket to give judgment in this matter!"

'"You good-for-nothing crowd!" exclaimed the basket. "Is this a profitable way to spend an evening? Would it not be much more sensible to put everything in the house in order, tidily? Everything ought to be in its proper place. I will draw up a list of instructions."

'"Let's bustle about!" they all cried together.

'At that moment the door opened, and in came the maid. Immediately they all stood still, and no one dared to budge. The maid took the matches and struck a light, and what a marvellous spluttering and glow of flame there was!

'Now everyone can see, thought the matches, that we are the most beautiful and most useful things in the house. How light and bright we are! But almost at once they had burnt out and died!'

'That was a wonderful story!' said the sultan's wife. 'I felt I was lying right beside the matches on the mantelpiece. Yes, you must marry our daughter.'

'I agree,' said the sultan. 'The wedding will take place next Monday.'

The whole city was brightly lit on the evening before the wedding. Bread and twisty rolls were distributed to the population, and urchins thronged the lanes and public streets, whistling and shouting. It was a magnificent occasion.

The young bridegroom thought he should make a small contribution to the festivities, so he bought rockets and all sorts of fireworks, which he took up with him in his magic trunk. They cracked and exploded and showered down bright sparks. The Turks had never seen such a marvellous sight.

When the young man had landed his magic trunk in the wood once more, he hid it carefully and set off on foot into town, to ask the people how his display had looked from below. They all had something different to say to him about it. Everyone seemed to have seen something which the others had not, but his show had undoubtedly made a great impression on them all.

'He is clearly a very powerful god!' said one. 'His eyes flashed like stars, and his beard was like a waterfall,' said another. 'He flew in a fiery cloak,' said a third, 'and pretty angel-faces peered out from the folds.'

It was surprising to hear all these strange tales about himself. And to think that he was to be married to the most beautiful girl on the very next day!

He returned to the wood, intending to lie down and rest in his magic trunk – but where was it? It was nowhere to be seen! Oh, horror – it had been burnt. A spark from one of the fireworks must have set it alight, and now there was nothing left but a tiny heap of ashes. Now he could no longer fly through the air, no longer reach his bride.

All day long the princess waited at the top of her tower for her bridegroom. Perhaps she is waiting there still.

And he? He roams the world and tells stories. But they are no longer as light-hearted as the tale of the matches.

Five in a Pod

Five peas lay together in a pod. They were green and the pod was green, and so they thought that the whole world was green, and that was quite right. The pod grew, and the peas grew. The sun outside warmed the pod, and the rain made it clear and translucent. As the peas grew bigger they began to wonder why they were lying in a row, and what would happen to them in the end.

'Are we to lie here for ever?' they said. 'We shall become quite hard if we stay here much longer. There must be something more exciting in store for us.'

Weeks passed by. The peas turned yellow, and the pod turned yellow. 'The whole world has turned yellow!' they declared, and they were quite right.

Suddenly they felt a jerk. The pod was torn from the plant, and stuffed into a coat-pocket, together with a number of other pods. 'Now we shall soon be opened,' they whispered expectantly.

'I am curious to see which of us will do best in the world,' said the smallest pea. 'Not long to wait now!'

Pop! The pod burst, and all five peas rolled out into the bright sunshine. They lay in a little boy's hand, and the little boy thought they looked just right for his pop-gun. He loaded the first pea and shot it into the air.

'Here I am on my way to seek my fortune,' cried the pea.

'I'm going to fly to the sun,' shouted the second pea, as he shot up into the sky.

'We are going to sleep,' said the third and fourth, 'just as soon as we fall to the ground.' And they fell from the boy's hand and rolled away. But the little boy picked them up and loaded them both together. 'We are going the furthest after all!' they cried.

88

'Who knows what will happen to me!' said the fifth, as he sailed through the air.

He landed on the rotting wooden sill of a little attic window, where he lodged in a crack filled with moss and soft brown earth. He lay hidden there for a long time, but not forgotten by God.

In the attic room lived a poor woman, who went out each day to earn her living. She cleaned out fire-places, swept rooms, scrubbed floors, and chopped wood; but even though she worked so hard, she was always poor. While she was out working, her little daughter stayed at home in the attic. She had been lying ill for a whole year, hovering between life and death. 'Perhaps she wants to join her sister with God,' said the poor woman. 'But I *do* want to keep her with me, if God will grant it.'

Early one morning the following spring the poor mother was about to leave for work. The sun was shining warmly through the little attic window, and the sick child was gazing at the sunbeams. Suddenly she noticed something, and cried, 'What is that green thing peeping up at the corner of the window-pane? It's waving in the wind!'

Her mother opened the window and looked out. 'Well!' she exclaimed. 'It is a little pea which has sprouted. How in the world can it have found its way up here? Now you have a little garden to look after.' And she moved her daughter's bed nearer to the window, so that she could look out at the little pea-plant more easily.

When the poor woman came home from work that evening, her daughter said, 'Mother, I think I am going to get well. The sun has been shining in on me all day, the little pea feels happy and is growing bigger, and I feel much better. I shall soon be getting up and going out into the fresh air.'

'Yes, of course, dear,' said the poor mother, grateful to the little pea for giving her daughter such happy thoughts.

She stuck a little cane into the wooden window-sill and tied the pea-plant to it, to prevent it from being broken by the wind. Then she stretched a length of thread from the window-sill to the roof, so that the tendrils could climb up it. Every day they could see the little pea-plant grow bigger.

'Oh, look!' cried the little girl one day. 'It has flowers!'

Indeed it had, and the mother began to hope that her sick child might recover. Certainly she looked a great deal better, particularly when she sat up in bed and watched the little plant, her eyes gleaming with excitement.

The following week the little girl managed to leave her bed for the first time, and she sat happily for a whole hour in the warm sunshine at the open window, tending her tiny garden of a single pea-plant. The delicate pink and

white blossom glowed in the sunlight and the little girl tenderly kissed the little green leaves.

The mother smiled happily at the plant, as though it were an angel from heaven. 'God must have made it grow here to fill us both with joy and hope,' she thought.

What happened to the other four peas? Well, the first one landed in the gutter. In a trice it was gobbled up by a pigeon, and lay inside its stomach like Jonah inside the whale. The two lazy peas, who had wanted only to sleep, fared no better, for they too were swallowed by pigeons. But all three were at least of some use in this way.

The pea who had wanted to fly right to the sun landed in a drain and lay soaking in the dirty water. Days passed by, and weeks and months, and it swelled, and swelled until it had almost reached bursting point. 'No pea could possibly grow bigger than me!' it exclaimed with pride. 'I must be the best of the five!' And the drain agreed.

But up at the attic window the little girl stood with sparkling eyes, and with the bloom of health on her cheeks. She cupped her hands tenderly round the delicate pea-blossom and gave thanks to God.

The Little Match-girl

It was snowing and the wind blew cold as darkness fell over the city. It was New Year's Eve. In the gathering gloom a little girl with bare feet padded through the streets. She had been wearing her mother's slippers when she left home, but they were far too big, and she had lost them while hurrying across a busy road. One of them was nowhere to be found, and a little boy had run off with the other. So now her bare feet were mottled blue and red with the bitter cold.

In her old apron the little girl carried bundles of matches

which her father had sent her out to sell, but all day long nobody had bought a single match from her. Cold and hungry, she made her weary way through the city. Brilliant lights streamed from the windows of big houses, where blazing fires crackled merrily in the hearth, and the smell of roast goose hung on the air, for it was New Year's Eve.

The little girl crouched down in a corner between two houses. She drew her knees up to her chest, but this seemed to make her even colder. She was afraid to go home, for she had sold nothing the whole day! Not a penny had she earned, and her father would surely be angry with her. But it was just as cold at home, for the wind whistled through the cracks in the walls and floorboards.

How wonderful it would be to light a match! All she had to do was to take one out of its bundle, strike it on the wall, and warm her fingers at the flame. She drew out a match and struck it. How it sparkled and gleamed! How the flames leapt and the shadows danced! It seemed to the little girl as if she were sitting by an enormous iron stove with brass ornaments on it. She stretched out her frozen feet to warm them – and the flame went out. Gone was the wonderful stove, and there she sat in the snow with the burnt-out match smoking between her fingers.

She struck another. The match flared up, making a new circle of brightness. The light fell on the stone wall, which immediately became as transparent as gauze. She found herself looking into a cosy room, where a table stood spread with a white linen tablecloth and set with silver, while in the middle steamed an enormous roast goose. The goose leapt out of the dish and began to waddle towards her – and the match went out. She saw nothing but the cold, grey wall before her.

Once again she struck a match, and found herself sitting at the foot of a magnificent Christmas tree. Thousands of tiny candles twinkled on the tips of the green branches, and brilliant paper streamers and tinsel hung down to the floor. The little girl stretched both her hands towards it – and the match went out. The candles seemed to climb higher and higher, until she saw that they were the cold, bright stars above her. One of them fell across the wintry sky, drawing a long fiery tail behind it. Someone must be dying, she thought, for her old Grandmother, who had always been so kind to her, had said, 'Whenever you see a falling star, you will know that a soul is on its way to God!'

She struck another match. It threw a warm circle of light all round her, and within the bright circle stood her grandmother, smiling gently down at her.

'Oh, Grandmother,' cried the poor girl, 'take me with you, please! I know I shall never see you again once the match burns out. You will vanish just as the warm stove, the roast goose, and the beautiful Christmas tree did!' Quickly she struck the remaining matches, one after the other, for she did not want her grandmother to disappear.

Never had her grandmother looked so kind. She gathered the little girl into her arms and swept her up to heaven. How bright everything was! Here she felt neither cold, nor hunger, nor fear – for they were with God.

Early next day the people found the little match-girl huddled against the wall, the spent matches scattered about her. She was dead – but there was a smile of happiness on her lips.

'Poor soul, she was trying to warm herself,' the people said; but no one guessed what beautiful things the little match-girl had seen by the light of her matches, nor how happy she was with her grandmother that glorious New Year's morning.

The Sunshade

Agatha was the daughter of a rich goldsmith, and lived in a grand house which had a great many rooms and sweeping staircases, and a fine, large garden. Her father gave her as many gold rings and bracelets as she wanted, and her wardrobe was full to overflowing with beautiful dresses of silk and bright satin. But she took no joy in all these things, for she was very ugly. All day she would wander about the house or pick flowers in the garden, not daring to go out into the streets until the dusk was falling.

One day the housekeeper who looked after the goldsmith's house fell ill and Agatha had to go to the market in broad daylight in order to buy meat and vegetables. She pulled her bonnet frills over her forehead, so that no one should see her ugly face, but the women in the marketplace all recognized her and whispered to each other, 'Look, there goes the goldsmith's daughter. It's true – she really is as ugly as they say!'

Agatha passed quickly between the stalls. She hated to hear people making fun of her, and wished she were safe at home.

Suddenly she heard an old woman calling after her, 'Where are you going in such a hurry, Agatha? Come and see my wares.'

The voice sounded kind enough, so Agatha paused and looked round.

'That's better,' said the old woman. 'Come here, my child. I have something to show you.'

She rummaged in an old hamper, pulled out a sunshade and opened it up. It was of delicate, pale-blue silk embroidered with tiny white pearls. 'Do you like it?' she asked.

'Oh yes,' replied Agatha. 'But I spend most of my time indoors, so I have no use for a sunshade.'

The old woman smiled. 'One moment,' she said. 'Hold the sunshade over your head and take a look at yourself!' A mirror gleamed in the old woman's wrinkled hand, and Agatha saw reflected in it the face of a beautiful stranger.

'There you are!' said the old woman. 'As long as you hold the sunshade over your head nothing but the beauty of your kind heart will be seen, and no one will dream of laughing at you.'

'If it were only mine,' the girl sighed, stroking the blue silk.

'It *is* yours, my child,' said the old woman. 'I have given it to you. Go now, and be happy.'

Agatha could see that the old woman was poor, and could ill afford to give presents, so she took a gold bracelet from her arm and handed it to her, saying, 'May I give you something too, to bring you happiness?'

So she went on her way. As she passed shyly through the market-place she felt the admiring glances of the passers-by, and she smiled happily under the blue dome of the sunshade.

As she entered the house she closed the sunshade, and once again she saw her ugly features looking back at her from the hall mirror. I will not tell Father anything about it, she thought. How sad he would be to see me beautiful one moment and ugly the next. So she hid the old woman's gift in a cupboard, and carried on with her work as though nothing had happened.

Before dusk fell Agatha put on a pretty silk dress and left the house. She did not care if people thought it strange for her to be carrying a sunshade when the sun had already set: she wanted to be beautiful! But everyone was so charmed by her loveliness that the sunshade went unnoticed. Long after she had passed by, people were still talking about the beautiful stranger.

There was a big park in the city, where a band played every evening beneath bright coloured lights. Agatha had always longed to join in the dancing there, but she had never dared. Now she felt no fear, and danced merrily beneath the fragrant acacia blossoms, gaily whirling the blue sunshade over her head.

All the young men of the city who had previously avoided Agatha now crowded round to talk with her, eager to know whether she were on a short visit to the city, or whether she meant to stay. She wandered happily past the fountains and through the rose-gardens with her admirers, talking and joking with sparkling eyes, until she heard a sudden burst of coarse, cruel laughter.

She stopped in dismay. Had the sunshade lost its magic power? Was she ugly again, and were the people laughing

at her? Surely not – all her companions were as attentive as ever. A moment later she saw that a crowd had gathered round a poor hunchback. People were tugging at his clothes and yelling, 'Go away! You're spoiling our fun, you ugly creature!'

'We must help him,' said Agatha. 'What harm has he done?' She forced a way between the dancers and said, 'Leave the poor fellow alone! Have you no thought for other people's feelings?'

'But just look how ugly he is,' shrieked a girl. 'The horrid dwarf!'

Agatha stood silent for a moment, and then she handed the old hunchback her magic sunshade. His features at once became youthful and bright, his back straightened, and he stood noble and tall. His persecutors stepped back in amazement. Agatha hung her head, thinking that all their scorn would now descend on her; but no one seemed to notice her, so astonished were they at the miraculous transformation of the ugly hunchback.

The man still held the sunshade over his head, unable to understand what had happened to him. Agatha held out her hand to take it back, but felt all at once that she no longer wanted it. Without a word she turned and walked away through the park. One by one the bright lights went out, but there was a full moon to light the paths, and the surface of the pond glittered between the silent banks. Agatha bent down to cool her brow with the cold water. But – was this her true reflection? A beautiful face, radiant with goodness, looked up at her from the deep mirror of the pond. It was even more beautiful than it had been under the sunshade. The stars twinkled in the water, and the breeze carried them on the waves, like thousands of little diamonds, to where Agatha knelt on the bank.

The Magic Horse

Many years ago there reigned a king of Persia called Sabur, who was the greatest and most powerful of all the rulers of his time. Every year he celebrated two festivals – Niraj, the feast of the New Year, and Mirjan, the feast of the autumn equinox. At these times he threw open his palaces to all his subjects, and set his prisoners free.

Now it came about that on one of these festivals an Indian sorcerer came to him with a priceless gift, a horse of blackest ebony, with trappings of gold set with precious stones. The king was most impressed with the skilled and delicate craftsmanship, but he could not help asking what was the use of such a creature.

'My lord,' replied the sorcerer, 'this horse can travel with its rider as far in one day as any normal horse can travel in a year, for it flies through the air.'

'By Allah,' said the king, 'if it is the truth you speak, I promise to grant you any request you wish to make.'

The sorcerer immediately swung into the saddle, and the horse rose several feet into the air. The king was delighted, and said, 'I see that you have spoken the truth. Now I must fulfil my part of the bargain. Name your reward.'

Now the sorcerer had heard that the king had a beautiful daughter. 'My lord and master,' he said, 'I should like your daughter as my bride.'

'So be it,' replied the king.

Meantime the princess had been standing behind a curtain and had heard everything. She had also seen that her husband-to-be was very old, with a face that was furrowed with a million wrinkles, while she was young

and graceful, dainty and gentle as a gazelle, lovelier than
the new moon.

The princess ran to her room and threw herself down,
weeping bitterly. And that is how her brother, Prince
Akmar, found her on his return from hunting. 'What is the
matter?' he asked.

'Alas, dear brother,' she replied. 'Our father intends to
give me in marriage to an ugly old sorcerer who has
deceived him with a magic gift. But I will not be his bride.
Can you not help me, brother?'

Her brother promised to do his best and hurried to his
father, the king. 'What is this I hear about a sorcerer?' he
said. 'And what is the present he has given you?'

'When you have seen the horse,' replied the king, 'you
too will be amazed.' And he ordered his servants to bring
the horse. The prince leapt nimbly into the saddle, and dug
his spurs into the horse's flanks; but the horse did not
budge from the spot.

The king called the sorcerer, saying, 'Show my son how

the horse works; then he will understand that I cannot refuse to grant your wish.'

The sorcerer quickly realized that Prince Akmar was no friend of his, and showed him a lever on the horse's right side. As soon as the lever was pulled, he said, the horse would take to the air. So the prince pulled it, and the horse took to the air and flew away, and soon it was only the tiniest spot in the distance.

The king was worried for his son's safety. 'How can he bring the horse back to earth?' he asked.

'My lord,' exclaimed the sorcerer angrily, 'is it my fault if you never see him again till the end of the world? He did not ask me how to bring it back to earth. I simply showed him what he *did* ask me.'

The king was greatly angered and had the sorcerer

thrown into prison. He tore the crown from his head, beat his breast, and wept. What a sad end to all the gay festivities! The palace gates were locked and bolted, and the whole city sank into the deepest mourning for the lost prince.

Meanwhile the prince had been carried up to the sun on the ebony horse, and was almost dead from the fierce heat. Before I faint away, he thought, I must look quickly to see if there is not a lever to make the horse descend. He reached with his hand down the horse's left flank, and there indeed was a second lever. He pulled it, and the horse began to descend. Soon the earth came into view, and the prince spied a great palace behind some trees. He flew the horse towards it and landed quietly on a balcony. By this time night was falling. He found a staircase which led downwards to a vestibule with walls of white marble. He looked about him and saw a light gleaming where a door had been left ajar. Softly he pushed the door open and took a few paces into the room. To his amazement the whole floor was covered with sleeping men, each with an unsheathed sabre at his side. From this he concluded that he was in the antechamber of a princess's boudoir, and that the sleeping men must be her bodyguard.

On tiptoe Prince Akmar approached a delicate silk curtain which hung over a doorway at the far side of the room. He lifted the curtain, and stepped into a cool, airy chamber. A number of low beds stood ranged round the walls, while in the middle of the room, set on a dais of white ivory, was a bed with hangings of rich silk. Here lay the princess, while her maids slept on the lower beds. Prince Akmar went quietly up to the princess, and pulled gently at her sleeve.

The princess opened her eyes. At first she was so surprised at the sight of a stranger in her boudoir that she was unable to utter a word. The prince took advantage of her

101

silence to bow his forehead until it touched the floor, saying, 'Most gracious princess, here at your feet lies the son of the King of Persia, brought here by a most extraordinary adventure, and now in deadly peril of his life unless you will be kind and generous enough to give him your help and protection.'

'Have no fear, dear prince,' replied the princess. 'Here in the kingdom of Bengal we respect the laws of hospitality just as you do in Persia.' With these words she wakened her maids, and ordered them to prepare food and wine for the prince, and to make a bed ready for him.

Prince Akmar slept long and soundly, and had just finished dressing himself next morning when the princess sent one of her maids to warn him that she was about to visit him. After mutual greetings he gave the princess a detailed account of his strange adventure. When he had finished, she said, 'Although I see you safe and sound before me, I feared for your safety all the time you were talking, until you told me how your horse landed so easily on the palace balcony.'

The prince was delighted that she was so sympathetic towards him, and asked her name. 'Shems al Nahar,' she replied, which means Midday Sun. They talked together happily for many hours, and it was no wonder that Prince Akmar soon became so enchanted by the beauty and grace of his hostess that he fell head over heels in love with her. Before nightfall he had confessed his love to her, and had asked her to be his bride. Nothing could have pleased her better, and as there was no reason to doubt that their parents would be delighted they saw no obstacle to their happiness.

The prince said he would like to take his bride to the Persian court the very next day, for he wanted to set his parents' mind at rest as to what had happened to him, and to win their approval for his wedding with the Princess of

Bengal. But although he assured her that the ebony horse travelled swiftly enough to take them to Persia and back in a single day, the princess insisted that he should first visit *her* father, to ask for her hand in marriage, as well as his permission to go to the Persian court.

They mounted the ebony horse together, and in next to no time they were in the king's palace. He gave them a great welcome, and raised no objection either to their wedding or to their immediate journey to Persia.

The sun had barely risen above the distant horizon on the following morning when the prince mounted the magic horse with his beloved, who clung to him as the horse took to the air. Soon they were high in the blue vault of the sky, travelling faster than the wind.

Three hours later they were over the capital of Persia. Prince Akmar brought the ebony horse gently to the ground in a garden outside the city. He helped the princess down and led her by the hand into a little summerhouse, saying, 'Wait here for a short while. I will go and tell my parents of our arrival. They will send the Vizir and the whole army in full regalia to welcome you to Persia.' And off he went alone.

He found his mother, father, and sister in robes of mourning for they were sure he had been killed. They ran to meet him with open arms, and asked amid tears of joy what had happened to him. Great was the rejoicing! The news of his return soon spread through the whole city, and the streets rang with shouts of jubilation. Trumpets sounded and cymbals clashed, and the mourning robes were changed for garments of rejoicing. The whole city was hung with banners and streamers, and thousands of people thronged the palace gates. The king ordered a week's festivities with banquets for all the people, and set all his prisoners free. Soon a joyful procession was on its way to the garden where Akmar had left the Bengali princess.

Meantime the wicked sorcerer, who had been set free with the other prisoners, swore a terrible revenge on Prince Akmar. He hurried on ahead of the procession and found the princess in the summerhouse, with the ebony horse tethered not far away.

The young prince crossed me because of his sister, he thought bitterly. Now I will repay him in his own coin and take away his bride on the ebony horse.

He knocked lightly on the summerhouse door.

'Who's there?' asked the princess.

'Your slave and faithful servant,' the sorcerer replied. 'Your prince has sent me to bring you to him. I am to take you to the palace on the magic horse, for Her Majesty the queen is eager to welcome you.'

The princess had not the slightest suspicion of his wickedness, and opened the door without a moment's hesitation. But when she saw the ugly and evil-looking old man she hesitated, and said, 'Has the queen no better servant than you to conduct me to her?'

'My queen has hundreds of fine-looking servants,' replied the sorcerer. 'But I am her oldest and most faithful servant, and so she sent me.'

The princess believed him, and mounted the ebony horse. The sorcerer mounted behind her and pulled the lever. The horse immediately rose into the air, circled round, and headed towards China.

At that very moment the procession from the palace arrived in the garden – the prince and princess with the king and the queen, followed by hundreds of troops arrayed in glorious colours, playing trumpets and beating cymbals and drums to welcome the Bengali princess to Persia. The prince stepped into the summerhouse to bring out his beloved. But the room was empty. In despair he flung his turban on the ground and began to beat his breast, and for a long time he would not be comforted. Then he thought to ask the gardener who else had been in the garden that morning. 'Only the Indian sorcerer,' replied the gardener.

Prince Akmar knew at once that the sorcerer had stolen his princess. But what could he do? He thought for some time, and then he turned to his father the king, saying, 'Go back to the palace. I do not yet know what I shall do, but I will not move from this spot till I have found a solution.' So the king and the whole procession turned and wended their way slowly and sadly back to the city. Rejoicing turned once more to mourning.

Meantime the sorcerer had reached China with the Bengali princess, and had landed beside a stream in a luxuriant green valley. 'Where is your master?' asked the princess. 'And where are his parents and sister?'

'Allah curse them all!' hissed the sorcerer. 'I am your master now. This is *my* horse – I made it. You shall never see your prince again. But do not fear. I have endless riches, and I will give you all the fine clothes you desire and fulfil your every wish.' He spoke thus, thinking to win her for his bride, but she would have none of him, and pushed him away with loud cries and weeping.

Now the Emperor of China was hunting in the valley at that time. He saw the poor girl weeping by the side of the stream, and wondered at her beauty. He kicked the sorcerer, who had fallen asleep, and asked, 'Who is this woman?'

'She is my wife, Your Majesty,' replied the sorcerer.

At these words the princess leapt to her feet and kissed the emperor's stirrup. 'He is lying, my lord. He is a wicked sorcerer who has deceived me and abducted me.'

'Seize the old man,' ordered the Emperor of China, 'and

throw him into my deepest dungeon.' And the emperor's servants carried out their lord's command.

The emperor turned back towards the city with the Bengali princess, and on the way he asked her to tell him about the ebony horse. 'Indeed, my lord,' she cried, 'it is a most wonderful horse, for it can travel great distances faster than the wind.' When the emperor heard that, he ordered his servant to put the horse safely in the imperial treasury.

The emperor was pleased and happy, and as soon as he reached his palace he had the princess shown to a magnificent chamber. That very evening he visited her, and told her that he wanted to marry her. The princess still thought of Prince Akmar, however, and would not listen to him. To escape his demands she pretended that she was mad. She beat her face with her hands, stamped her feet, and tore her clothes to the accompaniment of shrill cries.

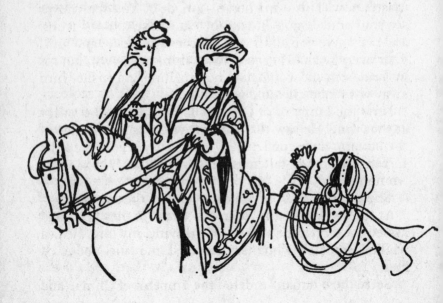

The emperor was sadly perplexed and left her apartment after giving instruction that she was to be carefully looked after by all his maid-servants, doctors, and astrologers.

Meanwhile Prince Akmar journeyed disconsolately from country to country, and in time the all-seeing and all-hearing Allah guided his footsteps to the capital city of China. In the bazaar there he heard the market-people talking of a beautiful girl in the palace who was out of her wits. He asked them how she had come to the palace, and when he heard their story he had little doubt that the girl was indeed his beloved.

He was overjoyed but cautious, so he disguised himself as an astrologer. He fashioned for himself flowing robes inscribed with magic symbols, and an immense turban for his head. He blackened his eyebrows and combed his beard, and altogether gave himself a most imposing appearance. He took a roll of fine parchment and a little box of sand, and presented himself at the palace. 'Tell the emperor that I am a wise astrologer, come all the way from Persia,' he said to the doorkeeper. 'I have heard of his slave's madness, and I am certain that I can cure it.' Quickly the doorkeeper let him in, and took him straight to the emperor.

Prince Akmar conducted himself like a real astrologer, muttering words which no one could understand, as he bowed deeply before the emperor and touched the ground with his forehead.

'Oh, wise one,' said the emperor, 'I have had the girl here for more than a year. She is for ever stamping her feet and beating the air with her arms, and nothing can make her stop. If you can cure her I will give you whatever you want.'

'Take me to her,' said the prince. 'First I must see her, in order to discover what manner of evil spirits have taken possession of her.'

The emperor ordered his servants to take the disguised prince into the princess's apartment, so that he might examine her. As he stood outside her door he heard the sound of weeping. He was sore at heart as he stepped quickly inside, and said, 'May Allah be merciful to you, Shems al Nahar! With his help you will soon be rescued. I am Akmar!'

As soon as she heard his voice the princess raised her eyes. With amazement and delight she recognized him through his disguise, and leapt to her feet. She threw herself into his arms and kissed him. 'But how in the world did you find me here?' she asked. 'There is no time to talk now,' he replied, 'for I still do not know how I am to take you away from here. But I shall soon find a way!' Reluctantly he turned and left her, and went back to the emperor. 'Your Majesty,' he declared, 'I will show you a miracle!'

The emperor rose and returned with Akmar to the princess's apartment. As soon as they entered she began to scream, and to brandish her arms and stamp her feet. Akmar went up to her and made magic passes with his hands over her face, and muttered incantations, whispering softly, 'Go quietly now to the emperor, kiss his hand, and show yourself compliant with his wishes.' After Akmar had made a few more magic signs with his hands the princess fell to the ground as if unconscious, and lay there motionless for several minutes. Suddenly she stirred as if she had just awakened out of a long sleep. Quietly she stood up, and went dutifully to the emperor, saying, 'Welcome, my lord and master. How gracious of you to visit your humble slave today!'

The emperor was beside himself with joy when he heard these words. He turned to the prince, and said, 'Ask for whatever you want. I grant it to you in advance.'

'No, Your Majesty,' replied the prince. 'It is not yet time

for my reward, for I fear the malady will break out afresh unless we act quickly. You must have her carefully bathed by ten slave-girls, but her feet must not be allowed to touch the ground. Then she must be arrayed in the costliest apparel, so that her heart will forget all its misery. And finally you must have her taken back to the place where you found her, for that is where the evil spirit entered into her.'

The emperor lost no time in carrying out the prince's advice. The whole court and the imperial guard followed the emperor, the prince, and the Bengali princess to the banks of the stream where she had first landed on her arrival from Persia. The prince muttered incantations, made mysterious signs with his hands, burnt incense, and watched the smoke formations as they rose into the sky.

After a while he approached the emperor, and said, 'Your Majesty, it is clear to me that the evil spirit which has taken possession of this woman belongs properly to a certain animal carved out of black ebony. Unless this animal can be found so that I can send the evil spirit back into it, I fear the lady cannot be properly or permanently cured of her madness.'

'You must indeed be the wisest of men,' said the emperor, 'the most brilliant astrologer I have ever met. For with my own eyes I saw a black ebony horse standing on the banks of this very stream where I first found the girl. Perhaps that is the animal which you have in mind?'

The emperor at once gave orders for the horse to be brought to him. The prince examined it carefully, in order to be quite certain that it had suffered no damage. Then he gave instructions for a ring of incense cones to be lit all round the horse. When all was wreathed in thick smoke Akmar lifted the princess on to the horse, leapt into the saddle before her, and pulled the lever. As the horse soared high into the air above the heads of the court, the emperor cried, 'Stop them! Stop them at once!' But what could anyone do?

Prince Akmar called down to him, 'Next time you want to marry a princess who has asked for your protection, do not forget to ask first if she wants to marry *you*!'

Swift as the wind they flew through the air, and in next to no time they landed on the steps before the palace of the Persian king. Like lightning the news of their happy arrival spread through the city, and all the people gave thanks to Allah, the All-powerful. All the citizens, the vizirs, and the royal troops turned out to welcome them and wish them joy. Messengers were sent to fetch the bride's father all the way from Bengal, and he brought with him many costly and beautiful presents for the happy couple.

The whole city was decked out with streamers and coloured lanterns. The wedding lasted for seven days and seven nights, and much money was distributed to the poor. The magic horse was put sagely in the royal treasury. But no one was quite so happy as the prince and his Bengali princess.

Puss in Boots

A miller had three sons, and when he died he left them his mill, his donkey, and his cat. The eldest son took the mill, and the second the donkey, leaving the youngest with nothing but the cat. The poor lad was most dissatisfied with his miserable share. 'If my two brothers stay together they can easily earn an honest living,' he grumbled. 'The mill will grind, and the donkey can be used to fetch the grain and carry away the flour. But when I have eaten my cat and made a pair of mittens out of its skin, I shall be left to starve.'

But the cat had understood perfectly all that he had said, although he had pretended not to hear. Now he said, 'Do not worry, master. Give me a sack and have a pair of boots made for me, and I will soon show you that your share of the inheritance is by no means as poor as you think!'

The miller's son had little confidence in these words, but he certainly remembered that on many occasions he had admired the cat's skill and prowess at catching rats and mice. So he did as the creature asked.

When the boots were ready the cat pulled them on, flung the sack over his shoulder, holding the strings tightly between his paws, and set off for Cotton-tail Hill, which was always swarming with rabbits. When he arrived there he put some lettuce leaves in the bottom of the sack, and lay down beside it as if he were dead, waiting for some young rabbit, inexperienced in the wiles of this world, to venture inside the sack and sniff the lettuce leaves. He did not have long to wait before a small rabbit lolloped up and crawled into the sack. Quick as lightning the cat pulled the string tight, seized the rabbit, and quickly killed it.

Feeling very pleased with himself he went to the royal palace and demanded to speak to the king. He was granted admission, and when at last he stood before the king he made a sweeping bow, and said, 'Most gracious Majesty, my master, the Marquis of Carabas, sends you this rabbit with his most humble respects, and beseeches you to accept it.'

'Tell your master,' replied the king, 'that I am most grateful to him.'

Next day the cat hid in a corn-field, where he caught a brace of partridges. He took them to the palace, and again the king accepted the gift with pleasure, handing the cat a generous reward. So it went on for two or three months. Each day the cat delivered some game to the king,

111

saying that it had been sent by his master, the Marquis of Carabas.

One day the cat discovered that the king intended to go for a drive in his carriage with his daughter, the princess. So he said to his master, 'Do not ask questions – just do as I tell you, and your fortune is made! All you have to do is to bathe at a certain bend in the river, which I shall point out to you, and I will see to the rest.'

The so-called Marquis of Carabas did exactly as the cat told him, without having any idea what the purpose was. While he was bathing, the king's carriage came bowling along, and the cat immediately began to call at the top of his voice, 'Help! Help! The Marquis of Carabas is drowning!'

The king stopped his carriage and put his head out of the window. He recognized at once the cat who had so often brought him game, and ordered his bodyguard to go to the rescue of the poor marquis. While his master was being hauled out of the river, the cat ran to the coach and told the king that thieves had stolen his master's clothes while he was bathing, although he had shouted at the top of his voice. (To tell the truth, the rascally cat had himself hidden the clothes under a stone, because they were all ragged and worn!)

The king was only too willing to show his gratitude to the kind marquis who had sent him so much game, and he ordered his footmen to fetch a suit of his own clothes for him. As the miller's son was a handsome young fellow, he looked a born nobleman in the fine clothes, with the result that the princess fell head over heels in love with him. The king meanwhile invited him to accompany them.

The cat was delighted with the success of his plan, and hurried on ahead. On the way he met harvesters cutting the corn, and said to them. 'Listen to me, good people. If the king asks you who owns this land, you must tell him it belongs to the Marquis of Carabas – otherwise you will all be chopped up into mincemeat!'

The king did indeed ask the harvesters who owned the land, and they all replied, 'The Marquis of Carabas, Your Majesty' – for the cat had put the fear of death into them.

'You have very fine lands, Marquis,' said the king.

'Quite good, Your Majesty,' replied the miller's son. 'The soil is excellent.'

The cat ran on in front, and came to some fields where harvesters were gathering and binding the sheaves. 'Listen to me, good people,' he said. 'If you do not tell the king that these fields belong to the Marquis of Carabas you will all be chopped up into little pieces.'

A few moments later the king drove by in his carriage, and wanted to know who owned the fine fields. 'The Marquis of Carabas,' cried all the harvesters, and the king was delighted to hear it.

On the cat ran in front of the carriage, and warned everyone he met to give the same answer, with the result that the king was soon amazed at the wide extent of the lands of the Marquis of Carabas. At last the cat arrived at a magnificent castle, which belonged to the real owner of all this vast estate. He was a rich ogre who terrified the whole neighbourhood, and lived on human flesh.

Now the cat knew all about the ogre, but he was not afraid, and asked to see him immediately. For, he said, he could hardly pass the castle without calling to pay his respects. The ogre received him kindly, as ogres can when they are in the mood, and invited him to sit down.

'I have been told,' said the cat, 'that you are able to turn yourself into any living creature you like – even a lion or an elephant. Is that true?'

'Yes, it is,' roared the ogre, 'and I can soon prove it to you.'

Suddenly the ogre vanished, and in his place stood an

enormous lion, swishing his tail and roaring so loudly that it seemed the roof would split. Scarcely had the ogre resumed his normal form than the cat jumped down from his chair, and pretended to be terrified, quaking in his boots.

'I have even been told,' he said, 'that you can turn yourself into the tiniest of creatures – for instance, a rat or a mouse – although I must confess that I find it very hard to believe.'

'You don't believe it?' exclaimed the ogre. 'I'll soon show you!' And that very instant the ogre turned himself into a tiny mouse, and began to scurry across the floor. That was just what the cat had been waiting for. With one leap he sprang on the mouse and gobbled it up!

At that very moment the king drew up to the castle. The cat had heard the royal carriage rattling over the draw-bridge, and ran out to bid the king a hearty welcome to the castle of the Marquis of Carabas.

'Aha, Marquis!' cried the king. 'Why did you not tell us it was your castle? It is the most wonderful building I have ever seen. Will you permit us to see the inner rooms?'

The miller's son helped the princess out of the carriage, and they went together into the lofty dining-hall. There they found a splendid meal set out, which the ogre had prepared for himself. The king became more and more delighted with the castle and its wide domains, and when he had drunk five or six glasses of wine and had eaten a little meat he turned to the miller's son and said, 'Well, Marquis, how would you like to marry my daughter?'

The miller's son bowed low and accepted the king's gracious offer without a moment's hesitation. The marriage took place that very evening, and the miller's son and his wife lived happily in the castle for many, many years.

The cat soon became a great country gentleman, and chased mice only occasionally – for amusement.

The Swine-herd

There once lived a prince who possessed only a very small kingdom. But his ambitions were big enough, particularly when it came to choosing a bride.

You may think him impertinent when you hear that he went straight to the emperor's daughter and asked her to be his wife. But it was not as bold as it seems, for many hundreds of princesses would have been only too willing to marry him. The emperor's daughter, however, was of a different mind.

Now on the prince's father's grave there grew a rose-tree which was different from any other rose-tree, for it bloomed only once in every five years, and then it bore only a single rose. The rose, however, had such a wonderful scent that whoever smelt it for a single second would forget all his cares and troubles. The prince also possessed a nightingale which sang the sweetest songs, as if it knew by heart all the lovely melodies in the world. When the prince set out to woo the emperor's daughter, he placed both the rose and the nightingale in beautiful caskets and sent them to the princess.

The emperor had the gifts taken into the great hall where the princess was playing hide-and-seek amongst the pillars with her ladies-in-waiting. When she saw the beautiful silver caskets she clapped her hands for joy, and ran to see what was in them, for she loved receiving presents.

'I hope it's a kitten!' she cried – and took out the magnificent rose. The princess touched the delicate petals, and almost burst into tears. 'What a shame!' she cried. 'It's an ordinary rose!'

'What a shame!' repeated all the ladies-in-waiting. 'Just an ordinary rose!'

'Let us see what there is in the other casket before we show our displeasure,' said the emperor as he took out the nightingale. It sang so beautifully that you would have thought no one could possibly find fault with it.

'*Superbe, charmant!*' the ladies-in-waiting cried out, for they all babbled away perpetually in bad French.

'This bird,' remarked an elderly courtier, 'reminds me vividly of the late empress's musical box. It has exactly the same tone, the same style of singing!'

'Yes, yes, you're right!' said the emperor, and burst into tears.

'It isn't by any chance a *real* bird?' asked the princess.

'Yes, it is a real bird,' replied the messenger who had brought the presents.

'Then let it fly away!' she cried. And she was so angry that she would not even allow the prince to come in and see her.

The prince, however, was not to be so easily put off. He plastered his face with mud, pulled his cap well down over his eyes, and knocked at the palace door.

'Good day, Your Majesty,' he said. 'Have you any work for me in your palace?'

'I doubt it,' replied the emperor. 'I have already more servants than I need. But wait! I *am* looking for a swine-herd. We have so many pigs here to look after!'

So the prince became the imperial swine-herd. He was given a miserable little hovel beside the pig-sties to live in, and there he sat all day long, working. By the time evening came he had made a lovely little cooking-pot with tiny bells hanging from its rim. As soon as the pot came to the boil the little bells began to ring, and played:

'Oh, my darling Augustine,
All is lost, all is lost!'

116

But that was not all – no, not by any means! When a finger was held over the steam it was possible to smell everything that was cooking in every house in the whole city. That was much better than a mere rose!

Now it happened that the princess was passing by with her ladies-in-waiting when she heard the sweet tinkling of the tune. She was entranced, and stopped to listen. It was the only tune she could play.

'That is my song!' she cried. 'What a clever swine-herd he must be! Go and ask him if he will sell the cooking-pot.'

So one of the ladies-in-waiting had to go and ask, though she took care to pull her galoshes over her slippers before entering the swine-herd's hovel.

'How much will you take for the cooking-pot?' she asked.

'Ten kisses from the princess,' he replied.

'God forbid!' cried the lady-in-waiting.

'As you wish,' said the swine-herd. 'But she will have to do without my cooking-pot.'

'Well, what does he want?' asked the princess, when her lady-in-waiting returned.

'I hardly like to tell you!' stammered the lady-in-waiting. 'It is too frightful!'

'Then whisper it to me,' ordered the princess, and the lady-in-waiting did as she was told.

'What a brazen fellow he is!' exclaimed the princess, and moved quickly on. Before they had gone far, however, they heard the little bells chime out again:

> 'Oh, my darling Augustine,
> All is lost, all is lost!'

'Go and ask him if ten kisses from any of my ladies-in-waiting would do instead,' said the princess.

'Oh no,' replied the swine-herd. 'Ten kisses from the princess or I keep my cooking-pot.'

'How frightful!' exclaimed the princess. 'Very well, I will do it – but you must all stand round me so that no one can see!'

So the ladies-in-waiting stood round the princess and spread out their skirts. The swine-herd received his ten kisses and the princess received her cooking-pot in exchange.

How pleased she was now! All the next day and throughout the evening the cooking-pot was continuously on the boil. There was not a house in the whole city where she did not know what was cooking, from the lord chamberlain's down to the cobbler's. The ladies-in-waiting danced and clapped their hands with delight.

'We know who is having broth and pancakes tonight! We know who is having meat puddings and who is having roast beef! How interesting!'

'Most interesting,' agreed the chief stewardess.

'Please don't give me away,' begged the princess. 'Remember I am the emperoror's daughter!'

'God forbid!' said all the ladies-in-waiting. 'We'll not whisper a word!'

The swine-herd – that is to say, the prince – did not let a day pass by without inventing something new. One day he made a little barrel-organ, and as soon as it was turned it played all the waltzes, jigs and polkas that have ever been heard since the world began.

'How beautiful!' exclaimed the princess as she was passing by. 'I have never heard such wonderful dance music. Go and ask the swine-herd how much the instrument costs. But remember, no more kisses!'

Before long, however, the lady-in-waiting whom she had sent returned to say that he wanted a hundred kisses for it.

'He must be quite mad!' declared the princess, and went

on her way. But she had not gone far before she stopped and said, 'I suppose I ought to do it for art's sake! I am the emperor's daughter after all. Go and tell him I will give him ten kisses, but the other ninety he must obtain from my ladies-in-waiting.'

'Oh, Madam! We cannot agree to that!' said the ladies.

'Nonsense!' said the princess. 'If I can kiss him, so can you. And remember, you depend on me for your board and lodging.' So the ladies-in-waiting had to return with this message.

'No,' said the swine-herd. 'I must have a hundred kisses from the princess, or I shall keep my barrel-organ.'

'Stand close round about me,' said the princess. So the ladies-in-waiting stood round in a circle, and the swine-herd began to kiss the princess.

'What is all that excitement down by the pig-sties?' exclaimed the emperor, who had strolled out on to the balcony at that moment. He rubbed his eyes, and put on his spectacles. 'Ah, as I thought! The ladies-in-waiting up to their nonsense again! I must go down and see what is going on this time!'

He quickly pulled on his slippers, and hurried downstairs. When he reached the courtyard, he crept up behind the little crowd as quietly as he could. The ladies-in-waiting were all far too busy counting the kisses to notice him, for they were determined that the princess should give neither more nor less than the hundred that had been agreed on. The emperor stretched up on the tips of his toes to see what was happening beyond the heads of the ladies-in-waiting.

'What is going on here?' he shouted, when he saw his daughter kissing the swine-herd. And he threw one of his slippers at them just as the swine-herd received his eighty-sixth kiss.

'Be off with you!' cried the emperor in a fury, and both

the swine-herd and the princess were banished from the kingdom.

The princess stood and wept, while the swine-herd grumbled and scolded, and the rain streamed down. 'What a wretched creature I am!' she sobbed. 'If only I had married the prince when he asked me I should not be so unhappy now!'

Hearing these words, the swine-herd quietly slipped behind a tree, wiped the mud from his face, threw off his ragged clothes, and stepped out – looking so handsome in his princely tunic that the princess at once made a deep curtsey to him.

'Yes,' said the prince. 'You see now who you have refused. But I have come to despise you! You would have nothing to do with an honest prince – you even disdained my beautiful rose and my precious nightingale – yet you found time to kiss a swine-herd for the sake of a mere toy. What you suffer now is no more than you deserve!'

With these words he turned and went back to his own kingdom, slamming the castle gates in her face. All the princess could do was stay outside and sing:

> 'Oh, my darling Augustine,
> All is lost, all is lost!'

King Thrushbeard

A king had an extremely beautiful daughter, but she was so proud and arrogant that no suitor was good enough for her. One after another they were laughed out of the palace in scorn. At last the king held a great banquet to which he invited anyone who wanted to marry the princess. All the suitors were drawn up in a line, in order of rank and social position; first came the kings, then the princes, dukes, counts, barons, and finally the noblemen.

The princess was led along the ranks, but she made some objection to each of her suitors. One was too fat, 'a beer barrel', she called him. Another was too thin, 'like a scarecrow', she said. A third was too short, 'a miserable dwarf'; a fourth was 'pale as a ghost'; a fifth was too red, 'just like a cock's comb!'; a sixth was too old, 'a green log dried at the fire'. She had some sharp words for every one of her suitors. The one who amused her most of all, however, was a good king whose chin was a little crooked. 'Do look at that!' she laughed. 'He has a chin like a thrush's beak!' After that he was known as 'Thrushbeard'.

The old king was very angry when he saw that she just made fun of all her suitors, and swore that she should marry the very first beggar to present himself at the palace door.

A few days later a wandering minstrel came to sing beneath the palace window, hoping to earn a few coppers. 'Bid him come up,' said the king, when he heard of it. So the minstrel came upstairs in his dirty, ragged old clothes, and played and sang for the king and his daughter. When he had finished he held out his hand for their charity. 'Your singing has pleased me so well,' declared the king, 'that I offer you my daughter to be your wife.'

The princess was dismayed, but the king told her that he had sworn she should marry the first beggar to present himself. He would not listen to her pleadings, but sent for the priest, who married them on the spot. After the ceremony was over the king declared, 'It is unseemly that a beggar's wife should remain in my palace, so off you go with your husband.'

The beggar took her by the hand and led her away, and she had no choice but to go with him, on foot. When they

came to a deep forest she asked, 'Who owns this beautiful forest?'

'It belongs to King Thrushbeard. It would have belonged to you too if you had married him.'

'How wayward and foolish I have been. I wish I had married King Thrushbeard!' she sighed.

Not long after, they crossed a wide meadow. 'Who owns this lovely green meadow?' she asked.

'It belongs to King Thrushbeard. It would have belonged to you too if you had married him.'

'How wayward and foolish I have been. If only I had married King Thrushbeard!' she sighed.

Soon they passed through a noble city. 'Who owns this fine big city?' she asked.

'It belongs to King Thrushbeard,' replied the beggar. 'If you had married him it would have belonged to you too.'

'How wayward and foolish I have been. How I wish I had married King Thrushbeard!'

'I do not like to hear you always wishing your husband were another man,' said the beggar. 'What is wrong with me? Am I not good enough for you?'

At last they came to a tiny hut, and she said, 'What is this miserable shack? Who owns this wretched hovel?'

'This is your house and my house, my dear,' replied the beggar. 'Take care not to bump your head in the doorway!'

'But where are all the servants?' asked the princess in despair.

'Servants?' answered the man. 'You must do everything for yourself here. Come on now, light a fire and prepare my supper quickly, for I am tired and hungry.'

But the princess had no notion how to lay a fire or cook, and the beggar had to help her. As soon as they had finished their meagre meal they lay down to sleep. Next morning he made her get up at the crack of dawn to do the housework. For a few days they muddled through in this way until all their food was used up. At last the man said, 'It can't go on like this, wife. We are eating and yet doing nothing to earn our food. You will have to weave baskets.' So out he went and gathered willows, which he brought home to her, and she tried to weave them into baskets, but soon her hands were cut and sore from the hard willows.

'This is not going to do us much good!' said the man. 'Perhaps you can spin better?' So she sat down and tried to spin, but the coarse thread cut into her soft fingers until they bled.

'This is not getting us very far either,' said the man. 'I have made a very poor marriage! What can you do? Let us try to start a pottery business – I will make the pots and plates and mugs, and you can sit in the market place and sell them.'

'Oh dear,' she thought, 'if people from my father's kingdom pass by and see me selling pottery, how they will

124

laugh at me!' But she had to do it if she was not to starve to death.

To begin with all went well, for the people were attracted by her pretty face and willingly paid what she asked for her wares. Many people even gave her money and left their pots with her. But one day as she sat surrounded by her pots and plates and mugs at the corner of the market, a drunken hussar came careering along on his horse and rode straight through her wares, shattering them into a thousand fragments. She burst into tears, terrified of what her husband would say. 'What can I do?' she cried. 'What will my husband say?' Home she ran and told him tearfully what had happened.

'Whatever made you sit at the *corner* of the market-place with pottery?' he exclaimed scornfully. 'Stop crying, woman. I see now that you are not fit for any kind of work. But I have been to the royal palace, and the king's chamberlain has promised you a place as a scullery maid. There at least you will be given your food.'

So the princess became a scullery maid and had to run after the cook and do all the dirtiest, greasiest and most unpleasant work. At night she went home with a little dish of left-overs in each pocket, and this had to do for their supper and breakfast.

The day came when the prince's wedding was to be celebrated in the palace, and the poor girl went and stood at the entrance to the great hall to watch. As the lights went up and the guests in their magnificent robes began to arrive, she cursed her pride and arrogance, comparing her own wretched fate and her poverty with the wealth and splendour which she saw displayed around her. From time to time the footmen would fling her a few left-overs and crumbs of the exquisite food they were carrying in and out, and these she stuffed into two little pots in her pockets to take home with her.

125

All at once the king's son himself approached her, dressed in velvet and silk, with gold chains about his neck. When he saw the beautiful young woman standing by the door, he took her by the hand to dance with her. She drew back in alarm, for she saw that he was the King Thrushbeard who had wanted to marry her and whom she had driven away with taunts and sneers. But her struggles were of no avail, and he drew her into the ballroom. The little pots fell from her pockets, so that the soup and left-overs fell all over the floor. What a shout of mocking laughter arose when the people saw it! The princess was so ashamed that she wished the earth would open and swallow her up. She turned and fled, but a man caught her on the stairs and brought her back. When she looked at him she saw that it was again King Thrushbeard.

'Do not be afraid,' he said gently. 'I and the beggar minstrel who married you are one and the same person. I was also the drunken hussar who broke up all your pots and plates with his horse. I disguised myself to rid you of your pride and arrogance, but I did it for love of you.'

She wept bitterly and said, 'I have done you great wrong, and I am unworthy to be your wife.'

'Be comforted,' he said. 'The days of sadness are over, and now we must celebrate our marriage.' Then ladies-in-waiting dressed her in magnificent robes, and her father was sent for. The entire court wished her great happiness in her union with King Thrushbeard, and so the true rejoicing began. I wish that you and I had been there too.

Robin Redbreast

In olden times there lived in the parish of Guirek in Brittany a poor widow called Ninorch Madek. She was the daughter of a rich nobleman, who, on his death, had left a castle and estate, a mill and a tile-kiln, as well as twelve horses and twice as many oxen, twelve cows and ten times as many sheep, not to mention the crops and the household linen.

But the poor widow's brothers, who should have protected their sister's interests, withheld her share of the inheritance. The eldest brother, Perrik, took the castle, the estate and the horses. Fanche, the second brother, took the mill and the cows. Riwal, the youngest brother, was given the oxen, the sheep and the tile-kiln. Nothing was left for poor Ninorch but a tumbledown hut without a door, out on the heathland, which once had been used as a shelter for sick cattle.

While the poor widow was moving her few household possessions into this miserable hovel, her brother Fanche seemed to take pity on her, for he said, 'I should like to deal kindly with you, so I am giving you this black cow. It is very thin and not very strong, and will hardly give enough milk to nourish a new-born child, so it is not much use to me. Keep it, and Mayflower can take it out to pasture every day.'

Mayflower was Ninorch's daughter, a child of eleven, as pale and as delicate as the white hawthorn blossom, and so it was that everyone called her Mayflower.

The widow took the cow, and sent Mayflower with it every day to the pasture. Mayflower would spend the whole day on the heath, tending the cow while it nibbled the few blades of grass that managed to grow on the stony soil. She would weave garlands of wild broom, praying aloud as she wove.

One day as she was singing a hymn which she had heard in the church at Guirek, she noticed a little robin perching on one of the garlands she had woven. It began to chirp, cocked its head on one side and looked at Mayflower as if it were trying to tell her something. She stepped a little closer to it, trying to make out what it was saying, but could not understand a word. The robin became almost frantic, fluttering its wings and hopping up and down at her feet, but she could make nothing of its twitterings. The tiny bird's antics so absorbed her that she did not notice the dusk falling. Stars were already twinkling in the sky when the robin took to the air and flew off into the night.

Quickly Mayflower ran to see what had happened to her cow, but she could not find it anywhere on the wide heath. She called at the top of her voice, rattled with her stick in all the bushes, climbed up to the little pools where the rain water collected, but all in vain. At last she heard her mother's voice in the distance, calling for her as if something dreadful had happened. She hurried to her mother, and found her not far from the hut, standing beside the cow's body, which had been torn and half devoured by wolves.

Mayflower was filled with sorrow at the sight. She fell on her knees and wept bitterly. Her mother tried to comfort her, saying, 'All creatures have to die some day, my dear. We are all at the mercy of wolves and wicked men, but God will protect us. Come, help me to gather my twigs and let us go home. What is done cannot be undone.'

Mayflower did as her mother bade her, but at each step she sighed deeply, and tears raced one another down her cheeks. She was so miserable that she could not eat a bite of supper, and she lay awake all night long, thinking she could hear the cow mooing at the door.

Next morning she rose early and hurried up on to the heath, barefoot and wearing only a thin cotton dress. On the same broom garland she saw the same little robin that had given her so much pleasure on the previous day. Once again it seemed to be trying to speak to her, but still she could make no sense of its twitterings. Angrily she turned to go, but suddenly she spied in the grass what seemed to be a gold coin. She placed her bare foot on it to feel it, but it was only a golden flower . . . a golden flower which could grant all those who trod on it barefoot the power to understand and to speak the language of the beasts of the field and the birds of the air.

Scarcely had she set her foot upon the flower than she began to understand exactly what the robin was saying to her. 'Mayflower,' it said, 'I have come to help you. Will you listen to me?'

'Who are you, then?' asked Mayflower, still astonished at finding herself suddenly able to understand the bird.

'I am Robin Redbreast,' answered the bird. 'I followed Christ to the Cross on Calvary, and with my beak I broke off a thorn which was scratching His brow. As a reward for this service God the Father lengthened my life until the day of judgment and gave me power to make one poor girl rich every year. For this year I have chosen you.'

'Is that true, Robin Redbreast?' said Mayflower joyfully. 'Then shall I be able to wear a silver cross round my neck, and shall I have enough money to buy myself a pair of wooden shoes?'

'You shall have a golden cross round your neck,' replied the robin, 'and wear a pair of silken shoes, as the noble-women do.'

'What must I do, then, dear bird, to earn this good fortune?'

'You have only to follow wherever I lead you.'

Mayflower followed wherever the robin led her, and so crossed the wide heath and came at last to the sand-dunes which faced the seven islands. There the bird stopped, turned to her and said, 'Do you not see something in the sand at your feet?'

'Indeed, I do,' said Mayflower. 'I see a pair of big wooden shoes and a staff of holly wood, untouched by any knife.'

'Put on the shoes and take up the holly staff,' ordered the robin. 'Now you must walk across the sea until you come to the first island. There you will find a great rock and a clump of sea-green rushes. Weave a rope with the rushes and strike the rock with your stick. A cow will come out. Throw your rope round her neck and lead her home to your mother.'

Mayflower did as the robin had said. She crossed the sea, wove the rope of rushes and struck the rock with her stick, and immediately a beautiful white cow appeared before her. Its eyes were as gentle as a spaniel's, its coat as shiny as a mole's, and its udder was soft with silky white down. How happy Mayflower was, and how happy her mother would be!

The robin had told her that the cow's name was Mor-Vyoch, which means sea-cow, because she had come out of the sea. When Ninorch tried to milk Mor-Vyoch the milk ran on and on through her fingers, as if it would never stop. Ninorch filled all her earthenware pots and dishes, then her wooden butter-churn and her tubs, and still the milk flowed.

'Dear Mother of God!' she exclaimed. 'When has a cow ever given so much milk?'

The sea-cow's milk seemed never-ending. She gave enough milk to feed all the children in the entire land. Soon everyone for miles around could talk of nothing but Ninorch's cow, and people came from far and near to see the wonderful animal. Even the priest came, for he wanted to be quite certain that the devil had no hand in the strange affair. But he had to admit that no mortal soul had anything to fear from the beast.

All the richest farmers round about wanted to buy Ninorch's cow, and each tried to outbid the other. Perrik, her eldest brother, came too, and said, 'If you are a good Christian, sister, you will not forget that I am your

130

brother, and will give me preference over all the others. Sell me Mor-Vyoch and I will give you nine cows in exchange.'

'Mor-Vyoch is worth far more than nine cows,' Ninorch replied. 'She is worth all the cows in this whole land! I can supply all the markets with milk, butter and cheese.'

'Very well, sister,' said Perrik. 'Give me the cow and I will give you the whole of our father's estate where you were born, the estate, with the cattle and everything else that goes with it.'

Ninorch accepted this offer, but not before she had been taken to the family estate and, following the ancient custom of Brittany, had dug a clod of earth, drunk water from the well, lit a fire on the hearth and cut a few hairs from the tail of every horse in the stables, to prove that she

owned all these things. Then she handed Mor-Vyoch over to her brother Perrik, who led the animal far away to a house which he possessed on the coast.

When Mayflower saw Mor-Vyoch being led away she burst into tears. Nothing would console her. At nightfall she went to the stables to see that there was plenty of hay in the mangers and water in the drinking-troughs, and as she worked she sighed, 'Why did they have to take the Mor-Vyoch away? When shall I ever see her again?'

Scarcely had the words left her lips than she heard a gentle mooing behind her, and as she understood the language of all animals she knew at once that it meant, 'Here I am!'

Quick as a flash she turned and saw the sea-cow standing there as large as life. 'Is it really you?' she exclaimed. 'Who brought you back?'

'I could not live with your Uncle Perrik. He is too heavily laden with sins. I belong to you, as before.'

'But does that mean my mother will have to give back the estate and all the horses?'

'Not at all!' replied Mor-Vyoch. 'The estate belongs to you, for your uncle deprived you and your mother of your rights in the first place.'

'But my uncle will return here to claim you.'

'Yes, indeed, so you must run quickly into the garden and pluck three sprigs of vervain. When you bring them to me, I will tell you what to do with them.'

Not a moment did Mayflower waste, and in a few moments she returned with the sprigs of vervain.

'Now,' said the sea-cow, 'you must rub me all over with the herb, from the tip of my tail to my horns, and repeat three times: "Saint Ronan of Hybernia".'

Mayflower did as she was told, and on the third repetition the sea-cow suddenly turned into a magnificent

132

chestnut horse! Mayflower's eyes almost popped out of her head.

'Will your Uncle Perrik be able to recognize me now?' asked the animal. 'Mor-Vyoch is no more. Now I am March-Mor.'

Next morning Ninorch wanted to try out the wonderful horse and send it to the market with some corn. What was her surprise to see that the more she loaded on to the animal's back, the longer its back became, so that it was able to carry a heavier load than all the other horses in the parish put together.

News of the wonderful horse soon spread far and wide, and before long it reached the ears of Fanche, the second brother. He came to inspect the horse, and offered to buy it from his sister, but she would not listen to him until he offered to give her in exchange the mill, with all the cows and everything else that went with it. Then she agreed to the exchange.

The bargain was concluded, and Ninorch took possession of the mill and Fanche took the sea-horse. But it was not yet evening when the horse returned to May-flower and told her once again to rub it from the tip of its tail to the tips of its ears with vervain and to repeat 'Saint Ronan of Hybernia' three times. In the twinkling of an eye, the horse changed into a beautiful sheep, heavily laden with rich scarlet wool, so long that it trailed on the ground, soft and shiny as spun flax. March-Mor was now Mor-Vauw, the sea-sheep.

Ninorch was astonished to see this new change, and called to Mayflower to fetch the shears. 'Look!' she said. 'The poor animal can hardly stand under the weight of its wool!'

She began to shear the fleece, but she had hardly begun when she discovered that the wool was growing almost as fast as she cut it. Her third brother, Riwal, passed that way as she was shearing, and he hastened to offer his tile-kiln and all his sheep as well as all the pasture-land in exchange for the wonderful animal. After a brief hesitation, his sister agreed.

But as Riwal was leading the sea-sheep along the coast it suddenly plunged into the waves and swam out to the smallest of the seven islands. The rock opened to admit the sheep, and Mor-Vauw returned no more to the land of men.

Next morning Mayflower ran out to the heath to find Robin Redbreast. 'I was waiting for you, my child,' he said. 'Mor-Vauw has gone, and will not return. Your mother's three brothers are well punished for their greed. You are now rich enough to wear a golden cross and silk shoes, as I promised you. My task is accomplished and I must fly far, far away. But never forget, my child, that you were once poor, and that a small bird made you rich, with the help of God.'

In token of her gratitude Mayflower built a chapel out on the heath, over the place where she had first met Robin Redbreast. And old men who heard this story from their fathers can remember worshipping in the chapel when they were children.

East of the Sun and West of the Moon

There was once a woodcutter who had a great many children, but he was so poor that he was barely able to feed and clothe them. The children were all fine-looking boys and girls, but the most lovely by far was the youngest daughter.

One Thursday night in late autumn, a fierce storm was

raging outside. It was pitch black, the rain streamed down in torrents and the wind howled and gusted until the windows creaked and rattled. The whole family was sitting round the fire when suddenly there came three loud raps at the window. The man went to the door to see who was there, and found an enormous white bear.

'Good evening,' said the bear.

'Good evening,' said the man.

'Will you let me have your youngest daughter to be my wife?' asked the bear. 'If you will, I can make you as rich as now you are poor.'

The man was pleased at the thought, but said he must first speak to his daughter. So he returned to the fire and said, 'There is a great white bear outside, who promises to make me as rich as now I am poor, if my youngest daughter will go with him as his bride.' But the girl said no, and would have nothing to do with it. The man went outside again and spoke kindly to the bear, telling him to return on the following Thursday evening.

The man and his wife tried hard to persuade their daughter, telling her of the riches that would be hers. At last she gave in, washed the few rags she possessed, dressed herself as neatly as she could and made ready for the journey.

When the bear returned on the following Thursday evening she was waiting for him with her bundle. She climbed up on to his back and they were away. After they had covered some miles, the bear asked, 'Are you afraid?'

'Not in the slightest,' she replied.

On and on they went, far through the dark night, until at last they came to a towering cliff. The bear knocked, and a door opened, admitting them to a great castle. They passed through brilliantly lit rooms, gleaming with gold and silver, until they reached a long hall, in which stood a table laden with sumptuous dishes. Here the bear handed the

girl a tiny silver bell, saying, 'If you want anything at all, just ring this bell.'

After she had eaten and drunk the girl felt tired and decided to go to bed, so she rang the little bell. Immediately a door opened to reveal a room, in which stood a delicately carved bed, with silken sheets and pillows and a gold-fringed canopy. She blew out the candle and lay down to sleep. A few moments later someone entered the room and lay beside her. This happened night after night, but the girl was never able to see who it was, for he never came before the light was snuffed, and always left before dawn each morning.

For a time the girl lived in this way, quite happy and contented. But at length she began to long for her parents and her brothers and sisters, and became silent and mournful. The bear asked her one day why she was so silent and downcast.

'Alas!' she replied. 'If only I could see my parents and my brothers and sisters again.'

136

'That can be arranged,' said the bear, 'but you must promise me faithfully never to speak with your mother alone, but only when others are present. She will try to draw you aside into another room, but if you give way to her you will make us both most unhappy.'

On Sunday the bear took her on his back and off they went. After they had travelled a long, long way, they came to a great white castle. Before it she saw her brothers and sisters playing. Everything was so splendid that it was a joy to behold.

'This is where your parents live now,' said the bear, 'but do not forget what I told you!'

'No, I will not forget,' replied the girl, and entered the castle. The bear turned and went away.

The parents were overjoyed to see their youngest daughter again and could hardly thank her enough for all she had done for them by agreeing to go with the bear.

'But how are you enjoying your new life?' they asked.

'All goes well with me,' she replied. 'I have everything I could possibly want.'

That afternoon, as the bear had foretold, the girl's mother tried to draw her aside into a separate room to talk. 'No,' said the girl, remembering the bear's warning, 'whatever we have to say can be said in front of the rest of the family.'

I do not quite know how it came about, but before her visit was over her mother succeeded in talking to her alone. The girl told her mother that each night, when she snuffed out the light, a man came and slept beside her, but that she had never set eyes on him, for he was always away before daylight. This saddened her, for she would so dearly have liked to see him, and the days were so long and lonely by herself.

'I am sure it must be a troll,' said her mother. 'Take my advice. Wait till he is sound asleep, and then light the

137

candle and have a good look at him. But take good care not
to drop any candle grease on him!'

That evening the bear came and fetched the girl away.
Before they had gone far, he asked her if things had not
turned out as he had warned.

'Yes,' she admitted, for she could not lie to him.

'Do not heed your mother's advice,' he warned, 'or you
will make both of us unhappy.'

'No, indeed,' she replied, 'I promise to be very careful.'

When they arrived at the castle in the cliff, the girl lay
down to sleep, and as before, when she had blown out the
light, the man came and lay down beside her. She waited
till he was fast asleep, and then got out of bed and lit the
candle. There in her bed she saw the most handsome
young man she had ever set eyes on, and she so loved him
that she could not resist the temptation to bend over and
kiss him. But she was careless and let three drops of hot
candle grease fall on his shirt so that he awoke with a
start.

'What have you done?' he cried, as he opened his eyes.
'Now you have ruined our happiness. If only you could
have waited for a whole year, you would have saved me! I
was bewitched by my step-mother, and I must spend the
hours of daylight as a bear and can become my true self
only during the hours of darkness. But now it is all over
between us. I must leave you and return to her. She lives in
a castle which lies east of the sun and west of the moon,
and there she will force me to marry a princess with a nose
that is three ells long!'

The poor girl burst into tears, but it was too late: he had
no choice but to go. She begged to be allowed to go with
him, but he said that could not be.

'Can you not at least tell me the way, so that I may look
for you?' she asked in despair.

'Yes, you can try,' he replied, 'but there is no road that

138

will lead you there. My step-mother's castle lies east of the sun and west of the moon. I fear you will never be able to reach it.'

When the girl awoke next morning both the young man and the castle had vanished, and she found herself on the bare earth in the heart of a thick, dark wood, with her poor bundle lying beside her. She rubbed the sleep from her eyes and cried till she could cry no more. Then she set out in search of the castle and wandered for many days, until she came at last to a high mountain. At the foot of the mountain sat an old woman playing with a golden apple.

'Can you show me the way to a castle which lies east of the sun and west of the moon?' she asked. 'A prince lives there, and he must marry a princess with a nose that is three ells long.'

'How do you know him?' asked the old woman. 'Are you perhaps the girl he wanted to marry?'

'Yes,' she replied. 'I am.'

'Ah! So you are the one!' said the woman. 'Then I should like to help you, my child, but all I know about the castle is that it lies east of the sun and west of the moon, and I fear you will never find it. But I will lend you my horse to take you to my nearest neighbour, who may be able to show you the way. When you reach her, slap the horse below the left ear and send it home to me. And take this golden apple with you – you may find it useful.'

The girl thanked the old woman, mounted the horse and rode for a long, long time. At last she came to a mountain at the foot of which sat an old woman with a golden spool. The girl asked her if she could tell her the way to the castle which lay east of the sun and west of the moon.

'I doubt if you will ever get there,' she said. 'But I will lend you my horse to take you to my nearest neighbour, who may be able to tell you the way. When you reach her, just slap the animal below the left ear and send it home to me. And take this golden spool with you – you may find it useful.'

The girl mounted the horse and rode for many days and weeks. At last she came to a mountain at the foot of which sat an old woman spinning with a golden distaff. Once again she asked the way to the castle which lay east of the sun and west of the moon.

'Are you the girl the prince wanted to marry?' asked the old woman.

'Yes,' the girl replied.

But the old woman knew the way no better than the other two. 'East of the sun and west of the moon,' she repeated. 'I fear you will never find it. But I will lend you my horse to take you to the East Wind – he may be able to help you. When you reach him, just slap the horse below the left ear, and send him back to me. And take this golden distaff with you – you may find it useful.'

The girl rode on and on and on, until she arrived at the

East Wind's dwelling. She lost no time in asking if he could tell her the way to the castle which lay east of the sun and west of the moon.

'Oh yes, I have heard of the prince, and the castle, too,' said the East Wind, 'but I cannot tell you the way, for I have never been so far. Let me take you to my brother the West Wind – he is much stronger than I. Perch yourself on my back and I will take you there.'

The girl jumped on to his back and off they went. When they reached the West Wind's dwelling the East Wind said that he had brought the girl whom the prince wanted to marry, and asked whether the West Wind could tell her the way to the castle which lay east of the sun and west of the moon.

'No,' said the West Wind. 'I have never blown so far. But, if you like, jump on my back and I will take you to my brother the South Wind. He is far stronger than I and blows far and wide.'

The girl jumped on to his back and it was not long before they reached the South Wind's dwelling. The West Wind lost no time in asking whether his brother knew the way to the castle which lay east of the sun and west of the moon, for the prince wanted to marry the girl he had brought with him.

'Indeed!' exclaimed the South Wind, but he did not know the way. 'I have blown far in my life-time, but I have never blown as far as that. But if you like,' he added, 'I will gladly take you to my brother the North Wind. He is the oldest and most powerful of us all, and if he cannot tell you the way I am sure no one can.'

The girl leapt on to his back and away they blew in such a gust that the earth trembled. In next to no time they arrived at the dwelling of the North Wind. But he was so wild and blustering that he hurled a blizzard of swirling snow and ice at them when he saw them approaching.

'What do you want with me?' he shouted in a voice which made their blood run cold.

'That is a fine way to greet your brother,' exclaimed the South Wind. 'I have brought a young girl to see you. She needs your help, for she is the girl who should marry the prince who lives in the castle east of the sun and west of the moon. She wants to ask if you know the way.'

'Yes, yes, of course I know the way,' said the North Wind. 'I once blew an aspen leaf there. The effort so exhausted me that I could not blow for weeks afterwards. But, if you are not afraid and are set upon going, I will take you on my back and see if I can blow you there.'

'Yes, I am determined to reach the castle,' said the girl, 'no matter what dangers beset us.'

'Then you must spend the night here,' said the North Wind, 'for we must have a whole day before us if we are to make the attempt.'

Early next morning the North Wind wakened her and blew himself up to such an enormous size that he was quite terrifying to see.

Then off they roared with a blast which seemed as if it would hurl them right to the end of the world. In the mighty hurricane whole villages and forests were destroyed. Across wide tracts of land and sea they raged, until it seemed they could go no further. At last the North Wind began to grow so weak that he scarcely had the strength to blow, and he sank deeper and deeper, until the waves were lapping about the girl's feet.

'Are you afraid?' he asked her.

'Not at all,' she replied.

By now they were not far from land, and the North Wind had just enough strength to set the girl down on the shore below the windows of the castle which lay east of the sun and west of the moon. The wind was so weak and exhausted that he had to rest for many days before he could journey home.

On the following morning the girl sat on the grass beneath the castle window and played with her golden apple. The first person to notice her was the long-nosed princess who was to marry the prince. 'What will you take in exchange for your golden apple?'

'It is not for sale,' replied the girl. 'Neither for gold nor silver.'

'Well, if you will not sell it for gold or silver,' said the princess, 'is there anything else you will take for it? I will give you whatever you ask.'

'You shall have it if I may sleep for one night in the prince's room,' said the girl.

'But of course you may!' exclaimed the princess, and took the golden apple.

When the girl entered the prince's room she found him deep in such a heavy sleep that she could not wake him, though she called him and shook him, and wept and cried. In the morning, as it was growing light, the long-nosed princess came and chased her out.

Again the girl sat down on the grass below the window and began to wind and thread on her golden spool. The long-nosed princess saw it, and asked the girl what she would take for it. 'It is not for sale, either for gold or silver. But, if I may spend another night in the prince's room, you shall have it.'

'Done!' said the long-nosed princess, and claimed the golden spool. But once again the girl found the prince so sound asleep that no amount of shaking and crying could rouse him. And in the morning, as it was growing light, the long-nosed princess again came and chased her out.

This time the girl sat on the grass below the window and spun with her golden distaff. When the long-nosed princess saw it she was filled with envy. She threw open the window and asked the girl if she would sell it. As before the girl answered, 'I will not sell it for gold or silver. But, if I may spend one more night in the prince's room, you shall have it.'

But some of the castle servants who slept near the prince's bedroom had heard for two nights the weeping and wailing of a woman coming from his room, and they had told the prince about it. So, when the long-nosed princess brought him his soup on the third evening, the prince pretended to drink, but poured it away behind him, for he guessed it contained a sleeping draught. That night, when the girl entered his room, she found him wide awake and overjoyed to see her. She told him all that had happened to her and how she had reached the castle.

'You have come at just the right time,' he declared, 'for tomorrow I am to be married to the princess. But what do I care for her – you are the only one I wish to marry! So I shall tell everyone that I want to see how clever my bride is, and shall insist that she washes the three spots of candle grease out of my shirt. She will agree to do it, but I know she is bound to fail, for these drops of grease can be removed only by a Christian hand – not by the hands of one of such a pack of trolls as owns this castle. I shall refuse to marry anyone who cannot remove the spots of grease, and when all the others have tried and failed I shall call you to try.'

Next morning when the wedding was about to take place the prince said, 'First I should like to see how clever my bride is. See, I have here a fine white shirt which I should like to wear for my wedding, but it is spotted with these three drops of candle grease. I have decided, therefore, to marry none but the girl who can wash out the grease.'

'What is so difficult about that?' murmured all the women.

The long-nosed princess set about washing the shirt, but the longer she scrubbed, the bigger and blacker the stains became.

'You're no good at it,' declared the old troll woman, her mother. 'Give it to me.' But no sooner had she laid hands on the shirt than it grew dirtier, and the more she rubbed and rinsed, the bigger the spots became. Then all the other troll women tried to wash the shirt, but the longer they washed, the filthier it grew. And finally the whole shirt looked as though it had been hung up in the chimney.

'Not one of you is any use,' declared the prince. 'But I see a poor beggar girl below the castle window. Perhaps she knows more about washing than all of you put together. Come on in!' he called. And when the girl came up he asked her, 'Can you wash this shirt clean?'

'I do not know,' said the girl, 'but I think I can.' She took the shirt and began to wash, and in her hands it became as white as driven snow – and even whiter.

'You are my true bride!' exclaimed the prince.

The old troll mother was so angry that she burst with rage; and the long-nosed princess and the whole pack of trolls must have exploded too, for I have heard nothing of them from that day to this.

The prince and his bride set free all the prisoners who had been held in the castle; and then they took as much gold and silver as they could carry and left far, far behind them the castle which lay east of the sun and west of the moon. How did they travel, and where did they go? That I do not know, but if they are the couple I think they are, they do not live far from here.

Wali Dad the Simple

There was once a poor old man called Wali Dad, who had no one in the world, neither wife nor children, and he lived by himself in a miserable little hut somewhere in the vast plains of India. Day after day he would go into the jungle to cut grass, which he could dry and sell as fodder for horses. He was a frugal old man and needed nothing but a little rice to eat, and so every day he managed to save half an anna, which he would throw into an earthenware chatti which he kept concealed in a hole in the floor.

One evening as he was finishing his scanty meal, he suddenly thought he would count his savings. With some difficulty he hauled the chatti from its hole in the floor, tipped the contents out on the table and stared in astonishment at the shining heap of coins.

What on earth could he do with all that money, he wondered. It did not occur to him to spend it on himself, for he was quite happy to spend the rest of his days as he had always done. So he flung the coins into an old sack, pushed it under his bed, and lay down to sleep.

Early the next morning he got up, slung the sack over his shoulder and staggered into the next town to a jeweller's shop, where he exchanged the money for a beautiful bangle of gold. He wrapped it carefully in his cummerbund and set out to visit a rich friend of his, a merchant who travelled about in many lands with his caravan of camels. Wali Dad was fortunate to find him at home, and after they had greeted one another and chatted about this and that, he asked his merchant friend if he could tell him who was the most beautiful and most virtuous woman he had ever come across on his travels.

After barely a moment's hesitation the merchant

146

replied, 'The Princess of Khaistan. The renown of her beauty, her virtue and her generosity has spread far and wide.'

'Well,' said Wali Dad, 'if you should visit Khaistan again on your travels, give her this golden bangle, with the most humble greetings of an old man in whose eyes kindness and goodness are worth more than all the riches in the world.'

With these words he took the bangle out of his cummerbund and handed it to his friend. The merchant was more than a little surprised, but he promised to carry out Wali Dad's instructions.

Soon after this the merchant set out on his travels once more, and after a time he came to the city where the princess lived. As soon as the opportunity presented itself he went to the palace and had the bangle delivered to the princess, laid in a beautiful, sweet-smelling box which he himself had provided. Nor did he forget to pass on Wali Dad's message to the princess. She could not imagine who could have honoured her with such a beautiful gift but she sent her servants to tell the merchant that she would be ready to send an answer as soon as he had finished his business in the city.

After a few days had elapsed the merchant returned to the palace, and the princess gave him a camel-load of costly silks as a present for Wali Dad, together with some money for himself. The merchant set out at once on the homeward journey.

It was some time before he reached his home, but as soon as he did so he went to see Wali Dad, to give him the princess's gift. The good old man was astonished to see a camel-load of silk rolling in at his door. What could he do with such luxuries? After a little thought he asked the merchant whether he knew of a young and noble prince who might be able to put his treasure to use.

'Yes, of course,' replied the merchant immediately. 'Of all the princes I know, from Delhi to Baghdad, there is none more noble or more worthy than the young Prince of Nekabad.'

'Excellent,' exclaimed Wali Dad. 'Then take him the silk, with the blessings of an old man.' He was happy to be rid of his treasure.

The merchant's very next journey took him to Nekabad, and after he had conducted his business in the city he requested an audience with the prince. When he was admitted into the royal presence he spread the magnificent silks at the prince's feet, and asked him to accept them as the gift of an old man who valued the prince's greatness and merit. The prince was moved by such generosity, and sent for twelve of his most beautiful stud-horses, for which his country was famous, and asked the merchant to present them to Wali Dad on his behalf. At the same time he gave the merchant a princely reward for his services.

The merchant hurried home and went straight to Wali Dad's little hut. When the old man saw the horses coming, he thought to himself, 'What luck! A whole troop of horses! They will eat cartloads of grass, and I shall be able to sell all I have without bothering to take it to the market.' And he hurried out to the edge of the jungle and started to cut grass as fast as he could.

When he returned, laden with as much grass as he could carry, he heard to his astonishment that the horses were his own. At first he stood perplexed, not knowing what to do, but then he had a sudden brainwave. He gave two horses to the merchant, and asked him to take the other ten to the Princess of Khaistan, who would doubtless find a use for such superb animals.

The merchant agreed with a laugh to do as his old friend wished, and took the horses to the princess's court. This

time the princess wanted to know more about the man who was sending her such costly gifts. Now, the merchant was most certainly an honourable man, but he hardly dared to describe Wali Dad as he really was – a wizened old man who earned a few annas each day and had hardly a rag to cover his back. So he told the princess that his friend had heard so much about her beauty and goodness that his heart moved him to lay the best things he possessed at her feet.

The princess had no idea how she should most fittingly respond to a man who showered such rich gifts upon her, so she took her father into her confidence and asked his advice.

'You cannot send his gifts back to him,' he replied. 'I think the best thing will be for you to send him so priceless a gift in return that he will be quite unable to match it. Then he will be ashamed, and will trouble you no more.' He ordered his servants to load twenty mules with silver, two mules for each of the ten horses, and to deliver them to the merchant, saying they were the princess's gift to Wali Dad.

So the merchant found himself suddenly in charge of a gleaming caravan. He had to take an armed guard with him to protect the caravan against robbers and marauding tribesmen, and it was a relief to him when he finally arrived at Wali Dad's little hut.

'Wonderful!' cried Wali Dad when he saw the treasures before his door. 'Now I can reply fittingly to the gift of the magnificent horses the prince sent me. But you, my friend,' he said to the merchant, 'you must have had to spend a great deal. If you will take six of these mules, together with their loads, and take the rest straight to Nekabad, I should be most grateful.'

The merchant was well aware that he was being most richly rewarded for his pains and agreed to set out for Nekabad immediately, for he was curious to see what course this strange affair would take.

This time the prince reacted as the princess had done. He was at a loss to understand why a complete stranger should send him such a rich gift. He asked the merchant what sort of a person Wali Dad really was, and in order to make his story ring true, the merchant could only praise Wali Dad's virtues so highly that the old man would certainly not have recognized himself, had he been present.

Just as the King of Khaistan had done, the prince made up his mind to send his unknown benefactor so kingly a gift that he would desist from sending further presents. So he had made ready a caravan of twenty pure-bred Arab horses with gold-embroidered bridles and silver saddles, twenty of his best camels, which could travel the whole day without tiring, and twenty elephants with pearl-embroidered silken covers and silver howdahs; and this great procession of animals was to be accompanied by a troop of men. What a fine sight it was, as they streamed across country.

When Wali Dad saw from afar the dust-cloud which this immense caravan raised, he said to himself, 'Here comes a great army of men, and elephants too! I shall be glad to sell all my grass to them!' And he ran to the jungle and cut grass as fast as he could. When he returned to his hut with the first load he found the enormous caravan and the merchant, who could hardly wait to show him the magnificent train and congratulate him on his vast fortune.

'Fortune!' cried Wali Dad. 'What can an ugly old man like me, with one foot in the grave, do with a fortune? Take it to the beautiful young princess – she would be able to enjoy all these beautiful things. Keep two horses, two camels and two elephants for yourself, with all their bits and bobs – and take the rest to her.'

At first the merchant made excuses and pointed out to Wali Dad that these journeys as messenger were causing him embarrassment. Certainly he was being richly rewarded for his pains, but he was tired of deceiving people. But the old man was so persistent that at last he relented. However, he determined not to let himself in for such an undertaking ever again.

After a few days' rest the great caravan set out for Khaistan. When the king saw the glittering train of animals streaming into the court-yard of his palace he was so amazed that he went down in person to see what it meant. When he heard that this was yet another present from Wali Dad to his daughter he scarcely knew what to say. He hastened to the princess's apartments and said, 'There seems little doubt, my dear, that this man is set upon marrying you. We have no alternative but to pay him a visit. He must be a man of immense wealth. And as he is so

151

devoted to you there seems little reason why you should not marry him.'

The princess agreed, and orders were issued to make ready a great train of elephants and camels, with silken tents and banners, litters for the ladies-in-waiting and horses for the men, for the king and his daughter were to honour the noble and generous Prince Wali Dad with a visit. The merchant was to guide the procession.

The poor merchant was now in a dire predicament! He was sorely tempted to run away, but as Wali Dad's ambassador he was received with such deference and hospitality in the royal court of Khaistan that he was never alone for a moment, and so found no opportunity to escape. After a few days he realized that he would have to submit to his fate, and only hoped that some act of providence would show him a way out of this awkward and embarrassing situation.

On the seventh day the royal procession set out, to the blare of trumpets and thunderous salutes from the palace guns. Day by day they drew nearer to Wali Dad's humble abode, and with each day the poor merchant felt more and more miserable. He wondered what kind of death the king would mete out to him, and suffered inward torture. Night after night he lay awake in his bed, racking his brains for a way out.

At last they were only one day's march from Wali Dad's hut, and the merchant was sent on ahead to warn Wali Dad of the approach of the king and princess with their train.

Wali Dad was busy preparing his meagre meal of onions and stale bread when the merchant arrived and told him what had happened. Wali Dad was so overcome with confusion that he burst into tears and began to tear his white hair. He implored the merchant to hold back the royal procession for one more day.

As soon as the merchant had departed it seemed clear to

Wali Dad that there was only one way out of the disgrace and despair he had brought on himself through his simplicity, and that was to take his own life.

Without saying a word to anyone about it, he went at midnight to a high cliff, at the foot of which the river wound through a deep gorge, and decided to throw himself down into the depths. When he reached the spot he walked a few steps back, took a run, and – came to a sudden halt on the very edge of the gloomy chasm. No, he could not do it!

Far beneath him, invisible in the darkness, he heard the water foaming and thundering over the rocks. The wind whistled mournfully through the gorge, and an owl fluttered and cried, 'Hoo! hoo!' close to his face. Terror-stricken, the old man shrank back from the edge of the abyss. He was frightened. Shuddering, he buried his face in his hands and began to weep loudly.

Suddenly he became aware of a soft, gleaming light flooding about him. Surely it could not be morning already? He took his hands from his face and saw two beings of unearthly beauty standing before him. They were spirits from Paradise.

'Why are you crying, old man?' asked one of them, in a voice as clear and sweet as the nightingale's.

'I am crying for shame,' he replied.

'What are you doing here?' asked the other.

'I came here to die,' he replied simply, and he told his story.

The first spirit approached him and laid a gentle hand on his shoulder, and Wali Dad felt as if something strange – he could not say what – was happening to him. His ragged old clothes were transformed into a beautiful embroidered robe, on his bare feet appeared soft, warm sandals and on his head a turban adorned with precious stones. About his neck hung a golden chain, and the old bent sickle, which he had cut grass with for years and which hung from his

belt, was suddenly changed into a gleaming sword with an ivory handle.

He stood bewildered, as in a dream, until the second spirit motioned to him to look round. What did he see? Before him a castle gate stood wide open and they walked forward along an avenue of huge plane trees. At the end of the avenue towered a magnificent palace, glowing with a thousand lights. On all the balconies and terraces servants hurried to and fro. The sentries strode up and down and saluted him respectfully as he approached. Wali Dad stood as though he had been struck dumb.

'Do not be afraid!' said one of the spirits. 'Enter into your house. Know that Allah rewards the simple and pure in heart.' With these words the two spirits vanished, leaving him alone.

Wali Dad went on, still as in a dream, and entered a great room more beautiful than any he had ever seen. Here he lay down to rest.

At first light he awoke and saw that the palace, the servants and all his fine clothes were reality, and knew that he had not dreamt it all.

Even more amazed than Wali Dad himself was the merchant, who came to him soon after sunrise. He told Wali Dad how he had lain sleepless all night, and had set out to see him at first light. But though he had searched he had been unable to find him. A great tract of thick jungle had been transformed overnight into beautiful gardens and parks. And if some of Wali Dad's servants had not found him and brought him into the palace he would have believed that he had gone mad and was imagining it all.

After Wali Dad had related all that had taken place that night the merchant hurried to the princess and the King of Khaistan, to conduct them to the palace.

The feasting in honour of the royal visitors from Khaistan lasted for three days and three nights. Every evening the king and his courtiers ate from golden plates and drank from golden goblets, and at the end of each meal the guests were asked to take the plates and goblets home with them as a token of remembrance. There had never been such a grand and glorious feast.

On the fourth day the King of Khaistan took Wali Dad aside and asked him if he wished to marry his daughter. Wali Dad replied that he would not have dared to dream of such an honour – he was far too old and ugly for such a beautiful young woman. However, he asked the king to stay on at the palace until he could send for his friend the Prince of Nekabad.

The king promised to do so, and next day Wali Dad sent the merchant to Nekabad with so many rich gifts that the prince could hardly refuse to come. As soon as he set eyes on the princess the prince fell head over heels in love with her, and they were married at once in Wali Dad's palace. There has never been, before or since, a grander or more sumptuous marriage feast.

When the celebrations were over the prince took his bride back to Nekabad, and the king rode home to Khaistan. Wali Dad lived on for many years and showed infinite kindness to all who were in need. And he always remained as simple and kind-hearted as he had been as a poor grass-cutter.

Beauty and the Beast

There was once a prosperous merchant who had six children – three boys and three girls. As he was a highly intelligent man himself, he insisted on all his children being well educated, and he engaged the very best tutors for them.

His daughters were all beautiful, but by far the loveliest was the youngest, who had been called Beauty from her earliest childhood. Truth to tell, her sisters were jealous of her because she had not grown out of the name. Besides, Beauty was more gentle and kind-hearted than her sisters, who were arrogant because of their great wealth. They liked to pretend they were great ladies and spurned the friendship of other merchant's daughters. They desired more select company. Day after day they would go dancing, to the theatre, or walking in the park, and they mocked their young sister, who spent most of her time reading good books.

Since it was well known how wealthy the family was, the sons of other wealthy merchants sought the three daughters in marriage. But the two elder sisters rejected them scornfully, vowing they would marry no less than a duke or a count.

But then the merchant lost his entire fortune, and all that remained was a tiny cottage in the country, miles away from the city. In tears he explained to his children what had happened and told them they must be prepared to work in the fields. At first the two elder sisters refused, saying that they still had a great many willing suitors in spite of their poverty. But they were mistaken for none of their former suitors would have anything to do with them now that they were poor. Indeed, many were delighted

that their pride and arrogance had been punished. 'They do not deserve to be pitied. Let them look after the sheep and still try to look like grand ladies,' they said.

At the same time, everyone was sorry for Beauty. 'What a dear, kind child she is! How good she was to all the poor people, how friendly and how gentle!' And, indeed, a great many young noblemen still wished to marry her even though she had not a penny to her name. But she always answered that she could not possibly desert her father in his misfortune; she would go with him to the country, to comfort him and help him in his work.

She was sad for her father's sake that all their money had gone, but she knew that no amount of crying would bring it back, and that it was quite possible to be really happy without great wealth or rich possessions.

In the country the man and his children worked hard in the fields to make a living. Beauty would get up at four in the morning to tidy the house and make breakfast. In the evenings, when the day's work was done, she would play the piano or sing as she worked at her spinning-wheel. The two elder sisters, on the other hand, were bored to death. They never got up before ten in the morning, never did a stroke of work on the farm, and spent all day lamenting their lost wealth and their fine clothes. 'Just look at our sister!' they exclaimed. 'That she can be happy in such miserable surroundings shows how stupid and vulgar she must be!'

Their good father, however, marvelled that Beauty was so patient with her two sisters, for not only did they leave her all the work to do, but they were ceaselessly scolding her and finding fault.

After the family had been living in solitude in the country for about a year, the merchant suddenly received a letter which told him that one of his ships had at long last come home to port safe and sound with all its cargo on board. The two elder sisters were overjoyed at the news, for they thought that they would now be able to leave the country, where they had been so bored. As their father made ready to set out for the port, they asked him to bring them dresses, furs, hats and all sorts of finery. Beauty did not ask for anything, for she knew that the sale of the whole cargo would not pay for half of what her two sisters demanded. 'Aren't you going to ask me to buy you anything, Beauty?' said her father.

'How good and kind you are to think of me,' she replied. 'May I ask you to bring me a rose, for we have none growing here?'

The merchant rode on his way: but when he reached the port he discovered that his goods just sufficed to pay his debts and no more. So he returned home as poor as when he had set out.

He had only thirty miles to go and was already looking forward to seeing his children again, when he lost his way in a great forest he was crossing. It was snowing heavily

159

and the wind blew in such gusts that twice he was blown from his horse. As night had already fallen he was afraid he might die of cold and hunger, or that he might even be attacked by the wolves which he heard howling all round him in the darkness. But then he caught sight of a light twinkling at the end of a long avenue of trees. He pressed on towards it and found that it came from a brilliantly lit castle. The merchant uttered a heart-felt prayer of thanks and hurried forward to investigate. To his astonishment he found not a soul inside, although all the lights were blazing. No one answered his shouts, and his horse – seeing an empty stable – trotted into it and helped itself eagerly to the hay and oats. The merchant went from room to room, but there was no one there. He came to a great hall where a huge fire blazed in the hearth and a table stood laden with roast meats, but with only one place laid.

The rain and snow had soaked the merchant to the skin, so he stood in front of the fire to dry himself and wait for the master of the house to appear. When the clock struck eleven and still no one had come, he decided he could wait no longer. Trembling, he helped himself to some roast chicken and a glass of wine. Emboldened by the food and warmth, he went through several more rooms, all magnificently furnished. Then he came to a bedroom with a fine, soft bed. It was past midnight and he was exhausted, so he closed the door and lay down to sleep.

He did not wake until ten the following morning, and when he rose he was astonished to find a fresh cloak in place of his old, threadbare one. 'Clearly this castle belongs to some good fairy who has taken pity on me!' he said. He looked out of the window and there was no snow to be seen. Acres of flowers met his delighted gaze.

He returned to the great hall where he had eaten on the previous evening. There he found a bowl of steaming hot chocolate waiting for him, so he said aloud, 'Thank you, my good fairy, for preparing me such a fine breakfast.'

After he had drunk his chocolate, the good man went out to fetch his horse. As he passed a rose-hedge he remembered that his youngest daughter had asked him to bring her a rose, so he broke off a spray with several fine blooms on it. At once he heard a great roar and turned to see such a fearsome monster approaching that he almost fainted with fear.

'You are most ungrateful!' roared the beast. 'I saved your life by taking you into my castle in the blizzard, and now you steal my roses, which I love more than anything in the world. You shall pay for this outrage with your life! I give you fifteen minutes to say your prayers and make ready.'

The poor merchant threw himself on his knees. 'Forgive me, my lord!' he begged. 'I had no idea I would be offending you by plucking a rose for my daughter.'

'Do not call me lord,' said the beast. 'Call me monster. I do not like flattery. I will forgive you on one condition – that one of your daughters will come here to die willingly in your place. Go now, and do not try to bargain with me. But before you go you must swear to return within three months, unless one of your daughters is willing to die for you.'

The good man did not intend to sacrifice any of his daughters, but he thought at least he would like to see his family again before he died. So he swore to return.

'Now you may go,' said the beast. 'But,' he added, 'I should not like you to leave here empty-handed. In the room where you spent last night you will find an empty trunk. Put into it anything you wish, and I will have it sent after you.'

With that, the beast left him, and the poor man thought that, if he had to die, at least he would be able to leave his children something. So he returned to the room where he had spent the night. There he found any number of gold coins, and with these he filled the trunk. Then he fetched his horse from the stables and left the castle as full of sorrow as he had been full of joy when he arrived. His horse soon found a way out of the forest, and within a few hours the merchant reached his home.

His children gathered round him, but instead of rejoicing in their welcome the merchant began to weep. 'Here, Beauty,' he said as he handed her the roses, 'take these roses. They have cost your father very dear.' And he related all that had befallen him. The two elder daughters began to scold Beauty, for she had not shed a single tear at his story.

'Why should I weep for my father's death?' Beauty exclaimed. 'He shall not die. The monster is willing to accept one of us in his place, and I shall be glad to prove my love by going when the time comes.'

162

'I am moved by your devotion, my daughter,' said her father, 'but I will not send you to your death.'

'I assure you, father,' she replied, 'that you shall not return to the beast's castle without me. You cannot prevent my following you. How could I live without you? I would much rather be devoured by the monster than die of sorrow because of your death.'

There was nothing her father could say to dissuade her. Beauty had quite made up her mind. Her sisters were delighted, for Beauty's virtue had roused their jealousy.

The merchant was so grieved at the thought of losing his daughter that he had quite forgotten about the trunkful of gold. But, as he was about to lie down to sleep that night, he saw to his astonishment that it was standing by his bed. He decided not to tell the children how rich he had become, for then they would have wanted to return to the city, and he had resolved to end his days in the country. He revealed his secret to Beauty, however, and she told him that several young noblemen had visited them during his absence and that two of them loved her sisters. 'Do let them be married, dear father,' she implored him, for her kind heart forgave her sisters all their faults.

At the end of the three months the merchant set off once more with a heavy heart, and with him went Beauty. Towards evening they reached the castle in the forest and found it as brilliantly lit as it had been the first time. The merchant took his daughter into the great hall where he found the table set for two and laden with appetizing dishes. The poor father could not bring himself to eat, but Beauty, who took great care to appear calm, sat down at the table and set food before him.

When the meal was over they heard a terrifying roar, and in tears the merchant bade his daughter farewell, for he knew that it was the beast. Beauty could hardly conceal her trembling when she saw the frightful monster, but she was calm once more when the beast asked her if she had come willingly. 'Yes,' she replied, with only a faint quiver in her voice.

'Thank you. You are very kind,' said the creature. 'Good man,' he continued to the father, 'you must leave this place at dawn tomorrow, and on no account are you to return.' And with these words the monster vanished.

'Oh, my dear child!' exclaimed the merchant, and kissed Beauty. 'Listen to me. Leave me here to die.'

'No, Father,' replied Beauty firmly. 'Tomorrow you must go and leave me to my fate. Perhaps the beast may take pity on me.'

They went up to bed, expecting to lie awake all night. But scarcely had they lain down than their eyes closed in a deep and peaceful sleep. Beauty had a vivid dream in which a strange woman appeared and said, 'My dear, you have a generous heart. Your kind action in giving your own life to save your father will not go unrewarded. Have no fear.'

When she awoke she told the dream to her father, and it comforted him a little as he took leave of his daughter, filled with sorrow.

Beauty sat down in the great hall and began to cry. But she was a courageous girl and she soon dried her tears, determined that she would not waste the short time remaining to her in vain regrets, for she believed the monster would devour her when evening came. She decided that she would have a good look round the beautiful castle. But how amazed she was when she came to a door with 'Beauty's Room' written upon it. She opened the door to look inside and was dazzled by the splendour of the room. But what she noticed above all was a marvellous library, a piano and a pile of music books. 'Well, they evidently do not wish me to be bored,' she said softly to herself. Then she thought that such great preparations would hardly have been made for her if she had only a day to live, and this thought cheered her.

She opened the book case, and her eye was caught by a book on which was written in gold letters: 'Wish. Command. You are queen and mistress here.' 'Oh,' she sighed, 'my only wish is to see my poor father and to know what he is doing now.' She did not speak these words aloud, but when her gaze fell on a large mirror she was astonished to see her home. Her father was coming sadly into the house and her two sisters were going to meet him. In spite of the faces they were making in their efforts to look sad and downcast, it was quite clear that they were glad to be rid of their youngest sister. Gradually the vision faded, but the castle now seemed warmer and friendlier and Beauty could not help thinking that perhaps the monster could not be so wicked.

At midday she found the table laid for her in the great hall, and as she ate she heard the most wonderful music, although there was no one to be seen.

As she was about to sit down to her evening meal she heard the roar of the monster, and she shuddered in spite of herself. 'Beauty,' he said, 'may I stay and watch while you eat?'

'You are master here,' she replied, trembling.

'No,' he replied. 'You alone are mistress here. You need only send me away if you find me a nuisance and I will leave at once. Tell me one thing – do you find me ugly?'

'I cannot lie,' answered Beauty. 'You are not beautiful, but I believe you are kind at heart.'

'You are right,' said the monster. 'But I am also stupid, for I am only a beast.'

'You cannot possibly be stupid if you think you are!' she replied. 'No simpleton ever realizes his stupidity.'

'Eat, Beauty,' said the monster, 'and try not to be bored in this house, for everything here belongs to you.'

'You are truly very kind. It seems to make you a little less ugly now that I know what a kind heart you have.'

'I may be kind-hearted,' said the monster, 'but I am still a beast.'

'There are many men who look more frightful than you,' continued Beauty, 'and I would rather have you, in spite of your appearance, than those who conceal a deceitful, selfish and ungrateful heart in a human form.'

Beauty enjoyed her meal. She had lost nearly all her fear of the monster, yet she almost died of fright when the beast said, 'Beauty, will you be my wife?'

For some moments she said nothing. She was afraid he would be angry if she refused, yet she said softly, 'No, good monster, I cannot.'

The poor creature sighed so deeply that the whole castle seemed to shake. But Beauty had no cause for alarm, for the beast said, 'Good night, Beauty. Sleep well,' and left the room.

Beauty spent three peaceful months in the castle. Every evening the monster would come to her and talk very pleasantly with her during dinner. She soon became quite accustomed to his ugliness and, far from dreading the hour of his arrival, she would find herself glancing at the clock to see if it were nearly nine o'clock, for he always came at that hour.

Only one thing troubled her: every night before going to bed the monster would ask her to marry him, and he seemed overwhelmed with grief when each time she said no.

One day Beauty said to him, 'You cause me great sorrow, my monster. I should like to marry you, but I cannot honestly lead you to hope that it could ever be. But I will always be your friend – try to be content with that.'

'I have no other choice,' replied the monster. 'I know

how fearsome I look, but I love you deeply. I am more than content that you will stay here with me. Promise that you will never leave me.'

Beauty blushed at these words, for she had seen in the mirror that her father lay ill with grief at losing his daughter, and she longed to see him again. 'I willingly promise never to leave you completely,' she said, 'but I long so desperately to see my poor father again that I think I shall die if you refuse me this joy.'

'I would rather die myself than cause you grief,' said the monster. 'I will send you home to your father, and you may stay with him, even though I know I shall die of longing.'

'No, no,' said Beauty, with tears in her eyes. 'I love you far too much, and I could not bear to be the cause of your death. I will return within eight days.'

'You will be home tomorrow morning,' said the monster. 'But remember your promise. As soon as you want to come back, lay your ring on the table before you go to sleep. Goodbye, Beauty!' As usual he sighed as he left the room and Beauty retired sadly to her bed.

When she awoke next morning she found herself in her father's house, lying in her own bed. She rang the little bell at her bedside and her father hurried in. His joy knew no bounds when he saw his dear child again.

When the first flood of joy was past Beauty suddenly thought that she could hardly get up if she had no clothes. But her father discovered a big trunk in the next room, full of golden, diamond-embroidered gowns. In her heart Beauty thanked the monster for his thoughtfulness.

She rose and dressed, and in the meantime her two sisters, who had been married and now lived most unhappily with their husbands, had been sent the news of her happy return. When they saw her, radiant in her loveliness and dressed like a princess, they almost expired with envy.

Although Beauty did her best to console them, their jealousy grew as she told them how happy she was. The two jealous sisters went out into the garden to conceal their annoyance, and the elder one said, 'We will keep her here longer than eight days. Her stupid monster will be so angry with her for not keeping her promise that he will be sure to devour her.'

'You are quite right,' agreed the other sister. 'But we shall have to be friendly with her if we are to succeed.'

When the eight days were up, the two sisters seemed so miserable at Beauty's impending departure that she agreed to stay for another week. And yet she reproached herself, for she knew well how the poor monster must be suffering on her account. On the tenth night she dreamt that she was in the castle garden and that the monster lay dying in the grass, reproaching her for her ingratitude. She awoke with a start and burst into tears. 'How could I be so wicked as to cause him pain! How can he help being ugly? He has a kind heart, and that means more than everything else. Why should I not marry him? I should be happier with him than my two sisters are with their husbands. It is not a man's intelligence or his good looks that make a woman happy, but his kindness and thoughtfulness.'

With these words she sat up, laid her ring on the table and then fell into a deep sleep. When she awoke next morning she found to her joy that she was once again in the monster's castle. She rose and dressed in her finest clothes to please him, and spent the whole day in desperate longing until at last it was nine o'clock. But when the hour struck, there was no sign of the monster.

Then Beauty was filled with fear that she might have caused his death. She ran sobbing through the castle, looking for the monster everywhere, until suddenly she remembered her dream. She ran to the stream in the garden, and there she found the beast lying on the ground

as though dead. Without the least fear she flung herself on
the body, but when she felt a flutter in the beast's heart she
scooped some water from the stream and sprinkled it on
his face. The monster opened his great, sad eyes and said
reproachfully, 'You forgot your promise. I was so heartbroken that I came here to die.'

'No, no, my faithful beast!' sobbed Beauty. 'You must
live and be my husband. I thought it was only friendship I
felt towards you. How wrong I was! Now I know that I
cannot possibly live without you!'

Hardly had the words left her lips than the whole castle
glowed with brilliant light. The strains of sweet music and
the joyful bursting of fireworks proclaimed a great feast.
But Beauty had no eyes for all this splendour. She turned to
her dear beast, full of concern lest he should die. But what
was her surprise! He had vanished, and at her feet she saw

a most handsome prince, who thanked her for having released him from enchantment. 'A wicked fairy condemned me to live as a beast,' he explained, 'until a beautiful girl would marry me. In the whole world only you were good enough to be moved by my own heart, and even if I offer you my crown, I shall never be able to repay the debt of thanks I owe you.'

Beauty lent the handsome prince her hand to help him to his feet, and together they went into the castle. Beauty could scarcely contain her delight on finding her father and her whole family in the great hall, brought there by the strange woman who had appeared to Beauty in her dream.

'Beauty,' said the strange woman, who was a powerful fairy, 'you are now rewarded for making a good choice, in preferring goodness and kindness to beauty and intelligence. You shall be a great queen, and I hope that the throne will not destroy your good qualities. As for you, my ladies,' she said, turning to Beauty's two sisters, 'I know your hearts and the wickedness they harbour. You shall be turned into a pair of statues, but beneath the stone you shall retain your understanding. You shall stand at the gates of the palace to witness your sister's good fortune, and you shall regain your human form only when you acknowledge your faults. But I fear you will remain statues for ever. Arrogance, ill-temper, laziness and greed can all be cured – but it is a true miracle if a wicked and envious heart repents.'

In that instant the fairy raised her wand, and everyone in the hall was transported to the prince's kingdom. His subjects welcomed him, full of joy, and he and Beauty were married and lived happily together for many, many years.

Dick Whittington and his Cat

A long time ago there lived in England a little boy called Dick Whittington. His parents had both died when he was tiny. He was still too young to work for a living, so he found life very hard. He had very little to eat, and on some days he had nothing at all. The people of his village were so poor that they could spare nothing at all, except potato peelings and an occasional dry crust of bread.

Now Dick had heard many strange things about the great city of London, for in those days the country folk believed that everyone in London was wealthy, that there was music and singing all day long and that the streets were paved with gold.

One day, as Dick was standing beneath the signpost, a great coach with eight horses, all wearing bells round their necks, rolled through the village. This coach must be going to London, he thought, so he plucked up courage and asked the coachman to let him run with the coach. Learning that Dick had neither father nor mother, the coachman felt that he could hardly be worse off in London than in the village, so he told him he could come along.

So Dick came safely to London, and he was in such a hurry to see the streets paved with gold that he did not even take time to thank the coachman properly. He ran along street after street as fast as his legs would carry him, and kept on thinking that the next street he came to would be paved with gold. Back in the village Dick had three times seen a gold sovereign, and he remembered what a heap of coins they had each been changed for. And so he thought that all he would need to do to have as much money as he would ever need would be to break off a little piece of gold from the pavement.

Poor Dick ran about until he was quite exhausted. Instead, of gold, all he saw in the streets of London was dirt. When darkness fell he curled up in a dark corner and cried himself to sleep.

Next morning he was ravenous. He ran from one person to another, saying, 'Please give me a ha'penny to buy a little bread.' But no one stopped to speak to him, and only two or three people gave him a ha'penny, so that poor Dick was soon weak and faint with hunger. In desperation he stopped all sorts of people to beg from them, and one of them said roughly, 'Why don't you work instead of loitering about, you idle good-for-nothing?' 'I should like to work,' replied Dick. 'May I work for you?' But the man only cursed and went on his way.

At last a kind-looking gentleman saw how hungry the boy was. 'Why don't you do some work, my lad?' he asked. 'I should like to work,' replied Dick, 'but where can I find it?' 'You can come with me and help with the haymaking, if you wish,' said the gentleman. Dick worked with a will until all the hay had been brought in and for a while things went well.

But after the haymaking he was as badly off as before. One day, desperate with hunger, he lay down at the door of Mr Fitzwarren, a rich merchant. He was soon found there by the cook, who was always in a bad humour. She was in the middle of preparing the midday meal for the merchant and his good wife, and shouted at poor Dick, 'What are you doing there, you lazy vagabond? We have too many beggars already. If you don't move on, I'll throw the slops over you – perhaps that will make you jump.'

At that very moment Mr Fitzwarren arrived home for his meal, and when he saw the ragged, dirty boy sitting at his door, he said, 'What are you doing there, boy? You look old enough to work. You must be a lazy good-for-nothing.' 'Not at all, sir,' replied Dick. 'I am not lazy and am only too eager to do some work. But nobody will give me any, and I think I am ill with hunger.'

'Poor fellow, stand up and let me see what is the matter,' said Mr Fitzwarren. Dick tried to stand, but immediately collapsed on the ground. He had eaten nothing for three days and was too weak even to beg for halfpennies. The good merchant had him carried into the house and given a good meal. After that he was told he could stay if he helped the cook.

Little Dick would have been happy in this household if the cook had not always been in such a bad temper. 'You're always under my feet,' she grumbled continually. 'Get on and clean the spit. Then you can scrub the pots and pans, light the fire and wash up. And be quick about it!' And she would fetch him a crack on the head with the soup ladle.

At length Mr Fitzwarren's daughter Alice discovered how badly the cook was treating Dick and warned her that she would be dismissed if she was not kinder to him. So the cook began to treat him a little better, but Dick had other discomforts to bear. His bed stood in an attic whose walls and ceiling were full of holes, and every night he was tormented by rats and mice. One day a gentleman gave him a penny for cleaning his shoes, and Dick decided to buy a cat. The very next day he met a little girl with a cat and asked if she would sell it to him for a penny. 'Yes, sir,' she said, 'but it's a real bargain, for she is an excellent mouser.'

Dick hid his cat in the attic and never forgot to take her some of his food. In a very short while there was not a rat or a mouse in the attic, and Dick could sleep peacefully at night.

Not long after this his master had a ship rigged out, and it lay in the harbour, ready to set sail. As it was the custom to offer all the servants the opportunity to make their fortunes on any voyage, Mr Fitzwarren called them all into his room and asked them if they had anything they would like to have sold or exchanged for them in foreign parts. Everyone had something except poor Dick. He had neither money nor possessions and so he did not go with the others to his master's room. Alice guessed the reason and sent for him.

'I should like part of my money to be his share,' she told her father.

'That is no use,' he replied. 'It must be something of his own.'

When poor Dick heard this he said, 'I have nothing but a cat, which I bought a while ago for a penny.'

'Fetch your cat, boy, and send her along to the ship.' So Dick went up to the attic and brought the cat down. With tears in his eyes he handed her to the captain and said, 'That means no more sleep at nights because of the rats and mice.'

Everyone laughed at Dick except Alice, who was sorry for him and gave him money to buy another cat. This and many other kindnesses which Alice showed poor Dick made the cook more and more jealous of him, and she began to treat him more harshly than before. She never stopped tormenting him, reminding him of how he had sent his cat to sea. 'Do you think the cat will fetch enough money to buy a stick to beat you with?' she said.

At length Dick could stand this treatment no longer and made up his mind to run away. He packed his few possessions together and slipped away early on the morning of the first of November, All Saint's Day. But he did not get further than Holloway. Here he sat down to rest on a stone, which is called 'Whittington's Stone' to this very day, and considered which road he should take.

While he was wondering what to do, he heard Bow Bells ring out loud and clear:

Turn again, Dick Whittington,
Thrice Lord Mayor of London.

'Lord Mayor of London!' he said to himself. 'Well, why not? It is worth putting up with a great deal if I am to be Lord Mayor in the end. Then, when I am a man, I can ride in a fine coach. All right, I'll go back and bear the old cook's cuffing and scolding until I am Lord Mayor of London.' Dick went back and, luckily, was hard at work before the cook came downstairs.

But now we must follow the travels of Miss Pussy to the coast of Africa. For many a long week the ship, with the cat on board, sailed the ocean, until the winds drove it ashore on the Barbary Coast, where the Moors lived. Crowds of people came down to the shore to stare at the crew, because they were a different colour from themselves. When they had got to know the captain and his crew they eagerly bought the fine wares with which the ship was laden.

When the captain saw this, he sent a messenger with the best goods he had to the king of the country. The king was most impressed and sent for the captain. He and his companions were given a gold and silver carpet to sit on, according to the custom of that country. The king and queen sat down to dine with them, but hardly had the food been brought in than score upon score of rats and mice appeared and in a twinkling devoured every morsel of food. The captain, in some surprise, asked the king if he did not find this plague of rats and mice very troublesome.

'Indeed, we do,' replied the king. 'I would give half my treasures to be rid of them.' The captain learned that not only did the rats and mice eat all the food, but that they worried the king at all times, even in bed at night, so that he had to set a guard in order to be able to sleep.

The captain almost leapt for joy, suddenly remembering poor Dick Whittington and his cat. He told the king that he had an animal on board his ship that would undoubtedly rid him of the plague of rats. When the king heard it he jumped so high for joy that his turban fell off. 'Bring me this animal,' he said. 'This plague is intolerable, and if your animal can really rid me of it I will gladly fill your ship with gold and precious stones.'

The captain, who knew his business, now praised all Miss Pussy's good qualities. 'I am not sure that I really ought to let the animal go,' he said to the king, 'for my own ship will be at the mercy of rats and mice if I have no cat on board. However, I shall be glad to fetch her for you to look at, if you wish.'

'Hurry, hurry!' exclaimed the king. 'I can hardly wait to see the animal.'

The captain ran back to the ship while another meal was being prepared. He tucked the cat under his arm, and arrived back at the palace to find the royal table seething with rats and mice. When the cat saw them she leapt from the captain's arms, and within a few moments nearly all the rats and mice lay dead, except for the few which had fled to their holes in fright.

The king was highly delighted to be rid of such a great plague so easily, and the queen asked for the cat to be brought to her so that she could see the amazing creature. So the captain called, 'Puss, puss, puss!' and took the cat over to the queen. But she took fright and drew back, not daring to touch the fearsome creature that had killed so many rats and mice.

The captain, however, stroked the cat and laid her on the princess's lap, where she played with Her Highness's fingers and then purred herself to sleep.

When the king had witnessed the heroic feats of which Miss Pussy was capable and had been told that her kittens would soon spread throughout his kingdom and keep it free of rats and mice, he bought the captain's entire cargo. But he gave ten times more for the cat than for all the cargo put together.

The captain then took his leave of the king, set sail for England with a favourable wind behind him and arrived safely in London within a few days of reaching port.

One morning, shortly after Mr Fitzwarren had entered his warehouse to begin the day's work, there came a knock at his door.

'Who's there?' he asked.

'A friend, good sir,' was the prompt reply. 'I have come to bring you good news of your ship.' The merchant rose in such a hurry that he forgot all about his gout, opened the door and – who did he see? His captain with a chest full of jewels! He could hardly believe his eyes, and thanked God for granting him such a successful voyage.

The captain told him the story of the cat and showed him the rich gift which the king and queen had sent for poor Dick. Mr Fitzwarren summoned all his servants to hear the glad tidings. One of his men suggested that such a vast treasure was too much for Dick, but Mr Fitzwarren proved his honesty and fairness in his reply. 'God forbid,' he said, 'that I should take so much as a penny of what belongs to Dick.'

Then he sent for Dick, who was busy scrubbing pots and pans and was dirty from top to toe. He begged to be excused, for his master's room was clean and his shoes were dirty. But the merchant insisted on his presence.

Mr Fitzwarren had a chair brought for Dick and told him to sit down. Dick thought they were all making fun of him, and said, 'Please let me go back to my work in peace!'

'I promise you, Mr Whittington,' said his master, 'we are in no way making fun of you. I am delighted at the wonderful news which has been brought by my captain, this gentleman here. He has sold your cat to the king of the Moors, and has brought in return a treasure that far exceeds my worldly wealth. May I wish you a long and happy life in which to enjoy it.' Then he ordered his men to open the treasure chest and show Dick his fortune.

Poor Dick scarcely knew what to do in his joy. He urged his master to take as much of it as he wanted, for he owed everything to his kindness and generosity. 'No, no!' replied Mr Fitzwarren. 'This is all yours, and I am sure you will use it well.'

Dick then asked his mistress and Alice to take part of his treasure, but they would not take anything. But he was far too unselfish a boy to keep it all for himself. He made a present to the ship's captain as well as to the crew and all Mr Fitzwarren's servants, even the cantankerous cook.

Mr Fitzwarren advised him to send for a tailor without delay and to have clothes made, fit for a gentleman of his wealth. And he asked him to remain in his house as a guest for as long as he liked, until he had found a house of his own.

When Dick had washed his face, combed his hair and

put on respectable clothes, he looked a remarkably handsome young man, and Alice, who had always been so kind, quickly lost her heart to him. Mr Fitzwarren saw that they loved one another and gave his consent to their marriage. The day of the wedding was soon set, and they were brought to church by the Lord Mayor of London and all the wealthy city merchants.

The story goes that Dick Whittington and his wife lived a long and happy life and that they had seven children. Dick became city magistrate, was three times Lord Mayor of London and was knighted by Henry V.

After the conquest of France he gave such a magnificent banquet for the king and queen that the king said, 'Never has a king had such a subject.' And when Sir Richard – for so Dick was now called – heard this, he replied, 'Never has a subject had such a king.'

Until the year 1780 the statue of Sir Richard Whittington, with his cat in his arm, stood over the arched gateway of the old prison at Newgate, which he himself had built for the prisoners.

The Emperor's New Clothes

Many, many years ago there lived an emperor who was inordinately fond of new clothes. He spent all his money on clothes and delighted in showing them off. He took no interest in his soldiers and bothered little about walking amongst his people or going to the theatre, except as opportunities for showing off his new clothes. He had a special tunic for each hour of the day, and whereas in most royal courts you would hear, 'His Majesty is in council,' in this court you would almost invariably hear, 'His Majesty is getting dressed.'

People led a merry life in the great city where he lived, and many strangers visited it. One day two swindlers arrived, posing as weavers and claiming to be able to weave the most beautiful cloth that could possibly be imagined. Not only were the colours and pattern of this cloth quite superb, they said, but any garments made of it possessed the unusual property of being totally invisible to anyone who was unfit for his post or incurably stupid.

What wonderful clothes they must be! thought the Emperor. If I had a suit like that I could soon tell who was stupid and who was intelligent, and which men in my court were unfitted for their posts. Yes, I must have some of this cloth woven for myself without delay! And he gave the two swindlers a generous advance to start work immediately.

They set up a pair of handlooms and pretended to be working at them, but they had no thread on the bobbins. They had the impertinence to insist on the most costly silk and the finest gold thread, but it all went into their own pockets, while they sat and worked at the empty looms until well into the night.

'I should like to know,' said the Emperor, 'how they are getting on with their work.' But to tell the truth he was a little frightened by the thought that a stupid or an incompetent person would not be able to see the material. Not that he was afraid for his own sake, but he felt that someone else ought to see and report to him before he looked for himself. By this time everyone in the whole city knew what wonderful properties the cloth possessed, and they were all curious to find out how stupid and incompetent their neighbours were.

I think I shall send my old Prime Minister to the weavers, thought the Emperor. He is quite reliable, he knows about weaving, he is intelligent, and no one is better suited for his post than he.

So the old Prime Minister went to the room where the two swindlers sat working at their empty looms. 'What on

180

earth!' he exclaimed, and his eyes almost popped out of his head. He saw quite clearly that there was no cloth on the looms, but he was careful not to say so.

The two swindlers told him to come closer, and asked his opinion on the beautiful pattern and brilliant colours, indicating the empty looms with their hands. The poor old Prime Minister stared and stared, but not a thing could he see – for the very good reason that there was nothing there. My goodness! he thought. Am I really so stupid and unfit for my post? I should never have believed it! I must take care that no one finds out! No, I cannot possibly admit that I cannot see the cloth!

'Well, what do you think of it?' asked one of the swindlers.

'Marvellous, quite marvellous!' declared the Prime Minister, looking through his glasses. 'What a wonderful design, and what superb colours! I must run and tell the Emperor. He will be delighted!'

'I'm glad you like it,' said the other swindler, as he proceeded to name the various colours and describe the intricate pattern. The Prime Minister listened with great care to what he was saying, so that he could repeat the description to the Emperor.

The swindlers demanded still more money, more silk and more gold thread for their weaving, and it all found its way into their own pockets. Not a single thread appeared on either of the looms, and yet they sat and worked away at the empty machines.

Soon after this the Emperor sent a second reliable minister to see how things were going and to report to him how his new clothes were progressing. The same sorry pantomime repeated itself. The minister stared and stared at the empty looms, but not a thing could he see but the bare wooden frames and the air beyond.

'Isn't it a fine piece of material?' asked the two swindlers

as they displayed on their arms a length of cloth which was not there.

Surely I cannot be stupid? thought the minister to himself. I suppose I must be unfit for my post. How dreadful! I must take care that no one finds out. Then, turning to the swindlers, he praised the superb colour and design. 'A glorious piece of material!'

By this time the wonderful cloth was almost the sole topic of conversation throughout the city. The Emperor decided that he must see it for himself while it was still on the looms, and went with a select company of his ministers to where the two swindlers were busy working away at the looms with bobbins but no thread.

'Isn't it wonderful?' asked the two ministers who had been there already. 'Do look at these gorgeous colours, and this beautiful design! Have you ever seen anything so splendid?' And they pointed to the empty looms, where they were convinced that everyone else could see more than they could.

This is dreadful! thought the Emperor. I cannot see a thing. Am I stupid, or am I unfit to be emperor? This is really most serious! But these thoughts he kept to himself. 'It is superb,' he said out loud. 'I am quite delighted with it.' And he peered closely at the empty loom frames, for how could he confess that he saw nothing? All his other ministers pressed forward to examine the cloth, and every one of them murmured, 'It is very fine!'

There was to be a great ceremonial parade in a few days' time and everyone advised the Emperor to have his new clothes completed as quickly as possible so that they should be ready in time for the great event. The Emperor was so pleased that he endowed the two swindlers with the title 'Weavers by appointment to the Imperial Court'.

On the eve of the great parade the swindlers sat up all night, apparently hard at work. All the lights were blazing, and anyone who cared to look could easily see that they were working their hardest in order to finish the new clothes in time. They could be seen evidently taking the material from the looms and cutting it with long scissors and sewing it with needles which had no thread. At last they declared that the clothes were ready.

The Emperor came at once with his most distinguished courtiers, and the swindlers held up their arms as if to display the garments. 'See, Your Imperial Highness,' they said. 'Here are the trousers, and here is your jacket, and is this not a superb cloak? Feel for yourself – they are as light as gossamer, you can hardly feel them. But that is the whole joy of them!'

'Yes, indeed,' said the courtiers, but not a thing could they see for there was nothing there to be seen.

'May it please Your Highness to try on these clothes,' said the swindlers. 'We should like to check the fittings in front of this big mirror.'

So the Emperor undressed and the swindlers went through the motions of dressing him, garment by garment, in his new clothes while he turned round and inspected himself in the mirror.

'What a perfect fit!' cried everyone. 'Have you ever seen such a superb costume? Such colours! Such a unique design!'

At this moment the Master of Ceremonies appeared, to announce that the canopy bearers were waiting outside to escort the Emperor to the parade. As he made the announcement the Master of Ceremonies bowed so low that his head almost touched the floor, for he had to conceal the smile that sprang involuntarily to his lips.

'I am ready,' said the Emperor. 'Isn't it a good fit?' Once again he turned in front of the mirror, for he wanted it to appear that he was full of admiration for his wonderful new clothes.

The footmen who were to carry his train fumbled about on the floor with their hands, as if to pick up the train. They walked behind him with outstretched arms as if they were carrying something, for how could they admit that they neither saw nor felt a thing?

So the Emperor stepped out of the palace beneath the magnificent silk canopy, and all the people who were gathered in the streets or clustered at the windows cheered, crying, 'What beautiful new clothes! Have you ever seen such a magnificent train?' For no one would confess that he saw nothing, as that would be admitting that he was either stupid or unsuited for his post. Never before had any of the Emperor's new clothes enjoyed such a tremendous ovation.

'But he has nothing on!' cried a small boy suddenly. 'Shush!' said his father. 'Just listen to the voice of innocence!' But it was too late, for by this time the whisper was spreading through the crowd: 'He has nothing on! He has nothing on!'

This annoyed the Emperor, for he felt that the people were right. But it could not be helped, he would have to brazen it out!

So he stepped out more majestically than ever, followed by his loyal footmen bearing a train which was not there.

The Happy Prince

High above the city, on a tall column, stood the statue of the Happy Prince. He was gilded all over with thin leaves of fine gold, for eyes he had two bright sapphires, and a large red ruby glowed on his sword-hilt.

He was very much admired indeed. 'He is as beautiful as a weathercock,' remarked one of the Town Councillors who wished to gain a reputation for having artistic tastes;

'only not quite so useful,' he added, fearing lest people should think him unpractical, which he really was not.

'Why can't you be like the Happy Prince?' asked a sensible mother of her little boy who was crying for the moon. 'The Happy Prince never dreams of crying for anything.'

'I am glad there is someone in the world who is quite happy,' muttered a disappointed man as he gazed at the wonderful statue.

'He looks just like an angel,' said the Charity Children as they came out of the cathedral in their bright scarlet cloaks and their clean white pinafores.

'How do you know?' said the Mathematical Master, 'you have never seen one.'

'Ah! but we have, in our dreams,' answered the children; and the Mathematical Master frowned and looked very severe, for he did not approve of children dreaming.

One night there flew over the city a little Swallow. His friends had gone away to Egypt six weeks before, but he had stayed behind, for he was in love with the most beautiful Reed. He had met her early in the spring as he was flying down the river after a big yellow moth, and had been so attracted by her slender waist that he had stopped to talk to her.

'Shall I love you?' said the Swallow, who liked to come to the point at once, and the Reed made him a low bow. So he flew round and round her, touching the water with his wings, and making silver ripples. This was his courtship, and it lasted all through the summer.

'It is a ridiculous attachment,' twittered the other Swallows; 'she has no money, and far too many relations'; and indeed the river was quite full of Reeds. Then, when autumn came they all flew away.

After they had gone he felt lonely, and began to tire of

his lady-love. 'She has no conversation,' he said, 'and I am afraid that she is a coquette, for she is always flirting with the wind.' And certainly, whenever the wind blew, the Reed made the most graceful curtseys. 'I admit that she is domestic,' he continued, 'but I love travelling, and my wife, consequently, should love travelling also.'

'Will you come away with me?' he said finally to her, but the Reed shook her head, she was attached to her home.

'You have been trifling with me,' he cried. 'I am off to the Pyramids. Goodbye!' and he flew away.

All day long he flew, and at night-time he arrived at the city. 'Where shall I put up?' he said.

Then he saw the statue on the tall column.

'I will put up there,' he cried, 'it is a fine position, with plenty of fresh air.' So he alighted just between the feet of the Happy Prince.

'I have a golden bedroom,' he said softly to himself as he looked round, and he prepared to go to sleep; but just as he was putting his head under his wing a large drop of water fell on him. 'What a curious thing!' he cried, 'there is not a single cloud in the sky, the stars are quite clear and bright, and yet it is raining. The climate in the north of Europe is really dreadful. The Reed used to like the rain, but that was merely her selfishness.'

Then another drop fell.

'What is the use of a statue if it cannot keep the rain off?' he said, 'I must look for a good chimney-pot,' and he determined to fly away.

But before he had opened his wings, a third drop fell and he looked up, and saw – Ah! what did he see?

The eyes of the Happy Prince were filled with tears, and tears were running down his golden cheeks. His face was so beautiful in the moonlight that the little Swallow was filled with pity.

'Who are you?' he said.

'I am the Happy Prince.'

'Why are you weeping then?' asked the Swallow; 'you have quite drenched me.'

'When I was alive and had a human heart,' answered the statue, 'I did not know what tears were, for I lived in the Palace of Sans-Souci, where sorrow is not allowed to enter. In the daytime I played with my companions in the garden, and in the evening I led the dance in the Great Hall. Round the garden ran a very lofty wall, but I never cared to ask what lay behind it, everything about me was so beautiful. My courtiers called me the Happy Prince, and happy indeed I was, if pleasure be happiness. So I lived, and so I died. And now that I am dead they have set me up here so high that I can see all the ugliness and all the misery of my city, and though my heart is made of lead yet I cannot choose but weep.'

'What! is he not solid gold?' said the Swallow to himself. He was too polite to make any personal remarks out loud.

'Far away,' continued the statue in a low musical voice, 'far away in a little street there is a poor house. One of the windows is open, and through it I can see a woman seated at a table. Her face is thin and worn, and she has coarse, red hands, all pricked by the needle, for she is a seamstress. She is embroidering passion-flowers on a satin gown for the loveliest of the Queen's maids-of-honour to wear at the next Court-ball. In a bed in the corner of the room her little boy is lying ill. He has a fever, and is asking for oranges. His mother has nothing to give him but river water, so he is crying. Swallow, Swallow, little Swallow, will you not bring her the ruby out of my sword-hilt? My feet are fastened to this pedestal and I cannot move.'

'I am waited for in Egypt,' said the Swallow. 'My friends are flying up and down the Nile, and talking to the large lotus-flowers. Soon they will go to sleep in the tomb of the great King. The King is there himself in his painted coffin. He is wrapped in yellow linen, and embalmed with spices. Round his neck is a chain of pale green jade, and his hands are like withered leaves.'

'Swallow, Swallow, little Swallow,' said the Prince, 'will you not stay with me for one night, and be my messenger? The boy is so thirsty, and the mother so sad.'

'I don't think I like boys,' answered the Swallow. 'Last summer, when I was staying on the river, there were two rude boys, the miller's sons, who were always throwing stones at me. They never hit me, of course; we swallows fly far too well for that, and besides I come of a family famous for its agility; but still, it was a mark of disrespect.'

But the Happy Prince looked so sad that the little Swallow was sorry. 'It is very cold here,' he said; 'but I will stay with you for one night, and be your messenger.'

'Thank you, little Swallow,' said the Prince.

So the Swallow picked out the great ruby from the Prince's sword, and flew away with it in his beak over the roofs of the town.

He passed by the cathedral tower, where the white marble angels were sculptured. He passed by the Palace and heard the sound of dancing. A beautiful girl came out on the balcony with her lover. 'How wonderful the stars are,' he said to her, 'and how wonderful is the power of love!'

'I hope my dress will be ready in time for the State-ball,' she answered; 'I have ordered passion-flowers to be embroidered on it: but the seamstresses are so lazy.'

He passed over the river, and saw the lanterns hanging to the masts of the ships. He passed over the Ghetto, and saw the old Jews bargaining with each other, and weighing out money in copper scales. At last he came to the poor house and looked in. The boy was tossing feverishly on his bed, and the mother had fallen asleep, she was so tired. In he hopped, and laid the great ruby on the table beside the woman's thimble. Then he flew gently round the bed, fanning the boy's forehead with his wings. 'How cool I feel!' said the boy, 'I must be getting better;' and he sank into delicious slumber.

Then the Swallow flew back to the Happy Prince, and told him what he had done. 'It is curious,' he remarked, 'but I feel quite warm now, although it is so cold.'

'That is because you have done a good action,' said the Prince. And the little Swallow began to think, and then he fell asleep. Thinking always made him sleepy.

When day broke he flew down to the river and had a bath. 'What a remarkable phenomenon!' said the Professor of Ornithology as he was passing over the bridge. 'A swallow in winter!' And he wrote a long letter about it to the local newspaper. Everyone quoted it, it was full of so many words that they could not understand.

'Tonight I go to Egypt,' said the Swallow, and he was in high spirits at the prospect. He visited all the public monuments, and sat a long time on top of the church steeple. Wherever he went the Sparrows chirruped, and said to each other, 'What a distinguished stranger!' so he enjoyed himself very much.

When the moon rose he flew back to the Happy Prince. 'Have you any commissions for Egypt?' he cried; 'I am just starting.'

'Swallow, Swallow, little Swallow,' said the Prince, 'will you not stay with me one night longer?'

'I am waited for in Egypt,' answered the Swallow. 'Tomorrow my friends will fly up to the Second Cataract. The river-horse couches there among the bulrushes, and on a great granite house sits the God Memnon. All night long he watches the stars, and when the morning star shines he utters one cry of joy, and then he is silent. At noon the yellow lions come down to the water's edge to drink. They have eyes like green beryls, and their roar is louder than the roar of the cataract.'

'Swallow, Swallow, little Swallow,' said the Prince, 'far away across the city I see a young man in a garret. He is leaning over a desk covered with papers, and in a tumbler by his side there is a bunch of withered violets. His hair is brown and crisp, and his lips are red as a pomegranate, and he has large dreamy eyes. He is trying to finish a play for the Director of the Theatre, but he is too cold to write any more. There is no fire in the grate, and hunger has made him faint.'

'I will wait with you one night longer,' said the Swallow, who really had a good heart. 'Shall I take him another ruby?'

'Alas! I have no ruby now,' said the Prince: 'My eyes are all that I have left. They are made of rare sapphires, which were brought out of India a thousand years ago. Pluck out one of them and take it to him. He will sell it to the jewellers, and buy firewood, and finish his play.'

'Dear Prince,' said the Swallow, 'I cannot do that;' and he began to weep.

'Swallow, Swallow, little Swallow,' said the Prince, 'do as I command you.'

So the Swallow plucked out the Prince's eye, and flew away to the student's garret. It was easy enough to get in, as there was a hole in the roof. Through this he darted, and came into the room. The young man had his head buried in his hands, so he did not hear the flutter of the bird's wings, and when he looked up he found the beautiful sapphire lying on the withered violets.

'I am beginning to be appreciated,' he cried; 'this is from some great admirer. Now I can finish my play,' and he looked quite happy.

The next day the Swallow flew down to the harbour. He sat on the mast of a large vessel and watched the sailors hauling big chests out of the hold with ropes. 'Heave a-hoy!' they shouted as each chest came up. 'I am going to Egypt!' cried the Swallow, but nobody minded, and when the moon rose he flew back to the Happy Prince.

'I am come to bid you goodbye,' he cried.

'Swallow, Swallow, little Swallow,' said the Prince, 'will you not stay with me one night longer?'

'It is winter,' answered the Swallow, 'and the chill snow will soon be here. In Egypt the sun is warm on the green palm-trees, and the crocodiles lie in the mud and look lazily about them. My companions are building a nest in the Temple of Baalbec, and the pink and white doves are watching them, and cooing to each other. Dear Prince, I must leave you, but I will never forget you, and next spring I will bring you back two beautiful jewels in place of those you have given away. The ruby shall be redder than a red rose, and the sapphire shall be as blue as the great sea.'

'In the square below,' said the Happy Prince, 'there stands a little match-girl. She has let her matches fall in the gutter, and they are all spoiled. Her father will beat her if she does not bring home some money, and she is crying. She has no shoes or stockings, and her little head is bare. Pluck out my other eye, and give it to her, and her father will not beat her.'

'I will stay with you one night longer,' said the Swallow, 'but I cannot pluck out your eye. You would be quite blind then.'

'Swallow, Swallow, little Swallow,' said the Prince, 'do as I command you.'

So he plucked out the Prince's other eye, and darted down with it. He swooped past the match-girl, and slipped the jewel into the palm of her hand. 'What a lovely bit of glass!' cried the little girl; and she ran home laughing.

Then the Swallow came back to the Prince. 'You are blind now,' he said, 'so I will stay with you always.'

'No, little Swallow,' said the poor Prince, 'you must go away to Egypt.'

'I will stay with you always,' said the Swallow, and he slept at the Prince's feet.

All the next day he sat on the Prince's shoulder, and told him stories of what he had seen in strange lands. He told him of the red ibises, who stand in long rows on the banks of the Nile, and catch goldfish in their beaks; of the Sphinx, who is as old as the world itself, and lives in the desert, and knows everything; of the merchants, who walk slowly by the side of their camels and carry amber beads in their hands; of the King of the Mountains of the Moon, who is as black as ebony, and worships a large crystal; of the great green snake that sleeps in a palm-tree, and has twenty priests to feed it with honey-cakes; and of the pygmies who sail over a big lake on large flat leaves, and are always at war with the butterflies.

'Dear little Swallow,' said the Prince, 'you tell me of marvellous things, but more marvellous than anything is the suffering of men and of women. There is no Mystery so great as Misery. Fly over my city, little Swallow, and tell me what you see there.'

So the Swallow flew over the great city, and saw the rich making merry in their beautiful houses, while the beggars were sitting at the gates. He flew into dark lanes, and saw the white faces of starving children looking out listlessly at the black streets. Under the archway of a bridge two little boys were lying in one another's arms to try and keep themselves warm. 'How hungry we are!' they said. 'You must not lie here,' shouted the watchman, and they wandered out into the rain.

Then he flew back and told the Prince what he had seen.

'I am covered with fine gold,' said the Prince, 'you must take it off, leaf by leaf, and give it to my poor; the living always think that gold can make them happy.'

194

Leaf after leaf of the fine gold the Swallow picked off, till the Happy Prince looked quite dull and grey. Leaf after leaf of the fine gold he brought to the poor, and the children's faces grew rosier, and they laughed and played games in the street. 'We have bread now!' they cried.

Then the snow came, and after the snow came the frost. The streets looked as if they were made of silver, they were so bright and glistening; long icicles like crystal daggers hung down from the eaves of the houses, everybody went about in furs, and the little boys wore scarlet caps and skated on the ice.

The poor little Swallow grew colder and colder, but he would not leave the Prince, he loved him too well. He picked up crumbs outside the baker's door when the baker was not looking, and tried to keep himself warm by flapping his wings.

But at last he knew that he was going to die. He had just enough strength to fly up to the Prince's shoulder once

more. 'Goodbye, dear Prince!' he murmured, 'will you let me kiss your hand?'

'I am glad that you are going to Egypt at last, little Swallow,' said the Prince, 'you have stayed too long here; but you must kiss me on the lips, for I love you.'

'It is not to Egypt that I am going,' said the Swallow. 'I am going to the House of Death. Death is the Brother of Sleep, is he not?'

And he kissed the Happy Prince on the lips, and fell down dead at his feet.

At that moment a curious crack sounded inside the statue, as if something had broken. The fact is that the leaden heart had snapped right in two. It certainly was a dreadfully hard frost.

Early next morning the Mayor was walking in the square below in company with the Town Councillors. As they passed the column he looked up at the statue: 'Dear me! how shabby the Happy Prince looks!' he said.

'How shabby, indeed!' cried the Town Councillors, who always agreed with the Mayor; and they went up to look at it.

'The ruby has fallen out of his sword, his eyes are gone, and he is golden no longer,' said the Mayor; 'in fact he is little better than a beggar!'

'Little better than a beggar,' said the Town Councillors.

'And here is actually a dead bird at his feet!' continued the Mayor. 'We must really issue a proclamation that birds are not to be allowed to die here.' And the Town Clerk made a note of the suggestion.

So they pulled down the statue of the Happy Prince. 'As he is no longer beautiful he is no longer useful,' said the Art Professor at the University.

Then they melted the statue in a furnace, and the Mayor held a meeting of the Corporation to decide what was to be done with the metal. 'We must have another statue, of course,' he said, 'and it shall be a statue of myself.'

'Of myself,' said each of the Town Councillors, and they quarrelled. When I last heard of them they were quarrelling still.

'What a strange thing!' said the overseer of the workmen at the foundry. 'This broken lead heart will not melt in the furnace. We must throw it away.' So they threw it on a dust-heap where the dead Swallow was also lying.

'Bring me the two most precious things in the city,' said God to one of His Angels; and the Angel brought Him the leaden heart and the dead bird.

'You have rightly chosen,' said God, 'for in my garden of Paradise this little bird shall sing for evermore, and in my city of gold the Happy Prince shall praise me.'

The Snow Queen

A Fairy-tale in Seven Stories

First Story

THE MIRROR AND ITS FRAGMENTS

Well, let's begin. When our story is over, we shall be wiser than we are now.

There was once a wicked goblin, the very worst of all, for he was the Devil himself. One day he was particularly pleased with himself, for he had just made a magic mirror which had the peculiar property of shrinking up everything good and beautiful that was reflected in it, and magnifying everything wicked and ugly out of all proportion. In this mirror the most beautiful views looked like mashed spinach, and even the best people looked repulsive in it or appeared to stand on their heads, with features distorted beyond all recognition. If a good man had a single freckle, the mirror would make it seem to spread all over his nose and mouth. And the Devil found this highly entertaining. If a man had a kind, generous thought, the mirror would show a ghastly leer on his face.

All his pupils, whom he instructed in the School for Goblins, spread abroad the news of the wonderful mirror, and declared that it showed the true face of the world and human kind. They carried the mirror all over the world, with the result that there was soon not a man alive who had not been sadly misrepresented in it.

Then they thought it would be fun to take it up to heaven and amuse themselves at the expense of God and his angels. The higher they flew with it, the more the mirror seemed to grin back at them till they found great difficulty in holding it fast.

Higher and higher they flew, nearer and nearer to God and his angels. At length the mirror quivered and shook so violently in its grimaces that it slipped from their grasp, and fell to earth, where it smashed into millions and millions of pieces.

In this way it caused more harm and suffering than ever before, for many of the splinters, hardly as big as a grain of sand, flew about in the air until they landed in somebody's eye. They made people see everything as distorted or, even worse, gave them eyes only for what was evil or ugly, for each splinter possessed the same evil properties as the mirror itself. But the worst damage of all occurred when someone caught a splinter in his heart, for then his heart became cold and froze to a lump of ice. Some fragments of the mirror were so big that they were used for window-panes, but it was a great misfortune to look into friends' houses through panes such as these. Some fragments were made into spectacles, and anyone putting them on saw everything distorted and was quite unable to tell right from wrong.

The Devil laughed till his stomach wobbled, so amused was he. There are still tiny splinters of glass drifting about in the air, and we shall hear more of these.

Second Story

A LITTLE BOY AND A LITTLE GIRL

In the big city, where there are so many houses and people that there is no room to spare for gardens and most people have to be satisfied with a few flowerpots, lived two poor children who none the less had a garden just a little bigger than a flowerpot. They were not brother and sister, but they were extremely fond of each other. Their parents lived in attic rooms which were right next door to one another. At the point where the roofs joined and the gutter ran between there was a little window in each attic. All the children needed to do to go from one window to the other was to step over the gutter. In front of each window there was a large wooden box where the herbs that were needed for cooking were grown, and a little rose-bush besides, one in each box, which flourished and grew. Then it occurred to the parents that it would be a good idea to place the window-boxes across the gutter so that they reached almost from one window to the other and looked as though they were two flowerbeds. Pea runners from the two boxes intertwined, and the rose-bushes joined over-head to form an arch of leaves and blossoms. From time to time the children were allowed to take their little chairs out on to the window-boxes, and they would sit beneath the roses and play together.

Winter, of course, put an end to this kind of fun, for the windows were often stuck fast with thick ice. Then the children would warm pennies on the stove and press them against the window-panes to melt a little peep-hole. How perfectly round these holes were! What fun it was to peep through and see another laughing eye looking back from a peep-hole in the opposite window!

The little boy was called Kay and the little girl Gerda. Outside swirled the snowflakes. 'There are the white bees swarming,' said Kay's grandmother.

'Do they have a queen bee, as ordinary bees do?' the boy asked.

'Yes, indeed,' replied his grandmother. 'She flies where the snowflakes swirl thickest. She is the largest of them all and never settles on the ground for long, but sweeps upward again to the black snow-clouds. On many a winter night she flies through the city streets, peering through the windows, which then adorn themselves with ice-flowers.'

'Oh yes, I have seen them!' cried the children, and now they knew that it was quite true.

'Can the Snow Queen come inside?' asked Gerda. 'Just let her come!' said Kay. 'I would put her on the stove and watch her melt.' But his grandmother stroked his hair and told him other stories.

That evening before going to bed, when little Kay was already half undressed, he climbed up on the chair by the window and peeped through the little peep-hole. Outside, snowflakes were falling, and one of them, the biggest, settled on the edge of the window-box. The snowflake grew bigger and bigger, until at last it turned into a beautiful woman. Her gown was of the finest white cambric and was scattered with millions of glistening, star-shaped snowflakes. She was dainty and slender, but made of ice, of pure, shimmering ice, and yet she was alive. Her eyes flashed like two bright stars, but there was neither peace nor repose in them. She nodded towards the window and waved her hand to him. The boy was frightened and jumped down from his chair. And then it seemed as if a great white bird flew past the window outside.

The following day the frost was severe, but soon afterwards it began to thaw, and spring followed shortly after that. The sun shone, the grass sprouted, the swallows built their nests, and once again the children sat together in their little garden high above the street.

That summer the roses were more beautiful than ever. Little Gerda had learnt a song about roses which reminded her of her own. She sang the song to her little playmate,

201

and he joined in. And the children held hands, kissed the roses and looked up into the glorious sunshine. What wonderful summer days those were! How delightful it was to sit up there so high above the street, beneath the fresh rose-bushes, which seemed as if they would go on blossoming for ever!

One day Kay and Gerda were sitting reading a book together – the clock in the great church tower had just struck five – when suddenly Kay cried out in pain. 'Oh, something has stabbed my heart! And I have something in my eye, too!'

Little Gerda flung her arms round his neck; he blinked his eyes but, no, there was nothing to be seen.

'Oh, it's all right now,' he said. But it was by no means all right. It was one of the glass splinters from the goblin's mirror – do you remember it? – the mirror that distorted everything good and beautiful, and magnified everything nasty and ugly? A sharp splinter had penetrated right into poor Kay's heart. It was no longer painful, but it was still there and it would turn his heart to ice.

'Why are you crying?' he asked. 'Crying makes you look ugly! I can't stand it. Ugh!' he exclaimed all at once. 'That rose has been eaten by worms. And that one is all crooked. How ugly all these roses are, and so is this whole window garden.' And with these words he kicked the boxes to pieces and tore down both the roses.

'Kay, what are you doing?' cried Gerda. And when he saw how horrified she was, he pulled off another rose, leapt through his own window and left poor Gerda outside on her own.

From now on, whenever she came to him with her picture-book, he would say it was fit only for babies. If her grandmother tried to tell them stories, he would scoff at them. He would even stand behind the old woman, with her glasses on his nose, and mimic her to make people laugh. Before long he could imitate perfectly the voice and mannerisms of everyone in the street, and people used to say, 'What a strange lad he is!' But it was only the glass splinters in his heart and eye that made him as he now was. For the same reason he would torment and tease little Gerda, who had never done him any harm. Even his games changed and became more serious than they had been before.

One winter's day when the snowflakes were falling, he poked a corner of his dark blue jacket out of the window to collect some snow-flakes and held a magnifying glass in his other hand.

'Look through the glass, Gerda,' he said, and he showed her how each snowflake was a perfect, ten-pointed star of dazzling beauty.

'See how perfect they are!' he exclaimed. 'How much lovelier they are than real flowers! If only they would not melt!'

Not long after this Kay came with his big gloves on his hands and his sledge on his back and yelled to Gerda, 'I'm off to play in the square with the other boys.'

One of the great games for the boldest boys in the square was to tie their sledges to the horse-drawn sleighs belonging to farmers from the outlying districts, and to go part of the way with them. What fun it was! While they were busy playing, a great white sleigh came gliding by, and in it rode a figure wrapped in a rough white fur, and wearing a white fur hat. The sleigh wheeled twice round the square, and the second time round Kay quickly fastened his sledge behind it and allowed himself to be pulled after it. Faster they went, faster and faster, from one white street to the next, and the white-shrouded form in front turned and waved to Kay, just as if they were old acquaintances. Every time Kay tried to loosen the rope the figure waved to him again, and he stayed where he was. On they sped through the city gates.

Now the snow fell thicker and faster than ever and Kay could hardly see his hand in front of his eyes. Faster and faster they flew, with the wind howling like a thousand demons in his ears. He called for help, but his cries were drowned in the frantic swirl of the snow. By this time the sledge seemed to be almost airborne and he could see ditches and dykes whipping past beneath him. Sheer terror held Kay in its grip and he tried to pray, but all he could say was his multiplication tables!

The snowflakes became bigger and bigger until at last they looked like great white hens. Suddenly the storm died down as quickly as it had begun, the sleigh came slowly to a halt and Kay saw the figure in front stand up. Hat and cloak were pure snowy white. It was a woman — tall, slim and dazzling white. It was the Snow Queen.

'We have made good time,' she said. 'But you are shivering with cold – come in under my bearskin cloak!' And she lifted him gently into her sleigh and wrapped him inside her cloak. He felt as if he were sinking into a snow drift!

'Are you still cold?' she asked as she kissed him. Her kiss was colder than ice and it seemed to pierce his heart, even though that was a lump of ice. He felt sure he was going to die – but only for a moment, for gradually he became less conscious of the intense cold.

'My sledge! Where is my sledge!' he cried, so the Snow Queen tied it to one of her great hens which flew behind the sleigh. She kissed Kay again, and this time he forgot all about Gerda and Granny and everything at home.

'I must not kiss you any more,' she said, 'or I shall kiss you to death!'

Kay looked up at her. She was indescribably beautiful. It

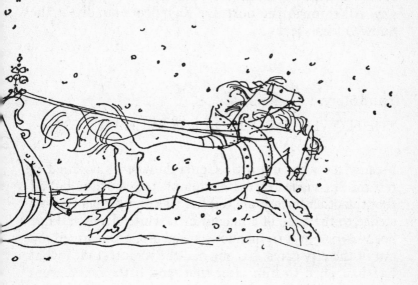

would have been hard to imagine more lovely and more intelligent features. No longer did she look as if she were made of ice, as she had done that time when she had sat outside his window and waved to him. No longer was he afraid of her. He chattered away happily, telling her how good he was at mental arithmetic, even fractions, how he knew the geography of the country and what the population was. How amused she was by his childish prattle! As she smiled at him, it struck him that perhaps he did not know very much after all.

High in the air they flew through the great black snow-clouds, while the storm whistled and raged about them and strange, haunting melodies filled the air. Over land and sea they flew, while down below them the bitter, cold wind blustered and the wolves howled. Now and then a huge raven would appear through the swirling snow and screech at them, only to disappear into the storm as suddenly as it had come. When darkness fell the storm abated and the silvery moon shone clear and bright in the sky. All through the next day Kay slept soundly at the Snow Queen's feet.

Third Story

THE FLOWER GARDEN OF THE ENCHANTRESS

Meanwhile what did little Gerda do when Kay failed to return? She made desperate attempts to trace him, but all that the other boys could tell her was that he had tied his sledge to the back of a magnificent white sleigh and had been carried at a tremendous speed along the street and out of the city gates. No one had the remotest idea what had happened to him after that, and little Gerda wept bitter tears. Most people were convinced that he must have been drowned in the river, but Gerda did not give up hope so easily.

What desperately long winter months those were! At last the first spring days came with their welcome blessing of warm sunshine.

'I suppose Kay must be dead!' sighed Gerda.

'Don't you believe it!' murmured a sunbeam.

'Surely he is dead?' she repeated, turning to the little swallows.

'What makes you so sure?' they replied. And at last Gerda's own hopes revived.

'I shall put on my beautiful new red shoes,' she said one morning, 'for Kay has never seen them. I must go and ask the river if it knows what happened to him.'

The first flush of dawn still glowed in the eastern sky as she gently kissed her sleeping grandmother, slipped on her new red shoes and went out through the city gates towards the river.

'Is it true that you took my little friend away from me?' she asked the river. 'I will give you my beautiful new red shoes if you will bring him back to me.'

It seemed as if the water swirled ever so slightly towards her, so she took off her red shoes, her most valuable possessions, and flung them into the river. But she had not thrown them very far and the water soon washed them up on the bank, as if to say that it knew nothing of Kay and would not deprive her of such lovely shoes. But Gerda was persistent. She climbed into a little boat which lay moored in the reeds in order to throw the shoes further out into the river. But the boat was not firmly tied and drifted quickly out into the current, and before she realized what was happening Gerda found herself being swept away downstream. She was terrified and began to call for help, but no one heard her cries. Her little red shoes bobbed merrily

207

along behind her, but they could not catch up with the boat.

How beautiful was the countryside through which she passed! Spring flowers and blossoming almond trees lined the banks, while sheep and cows grazed on the gentle green slopes beyond.

Gerda took courage from the hope that perhaps the river had accepted her gift after all and was taking her to Kay. After some time she came to a great garden full of flowers and cherry trees, in the midst of which stood a pretty little house with curious red and blue windows and a thatched roof. By the door stood two little wooden soldiers, who presented arms as she drew near. She called to them, for at first she thought they were real people, but not unnaturally they made no reply.

The river carried the boat quite close to the bank, and Gerda called again for help. This time a wrinkled old woman came out of the house, leaning on a crutch and wearing an immense straw hat whose brim was painted with all sorts of flowers.

'My poor child!' cried the old woman. 'What in the world are you doing on such a dangerous river?' She waded into the swirling waters and caught the boat with her crutch, brought it to the bank and helped Gerda to step out on to dry land.

Gerda was delighted to feel firm ground beneath her feet, but she was a little afraid of the old woman, who said, 'Come now, and tell me who you are and where you have come from.'

So Gerda told her the whole story and asked if by any chance the old woman had seen Kay. She replied that she had seen no sign of him yet, but that doubtless he would turn up. Meantime, Gerda was to stay with her, and pick the flowers and eat the cherries when they were ripe. Were her flowers not much more beautiful than the ones in

Gerda's picture-book? She took Gerda by the hand and led her into the house and closed the door.

'For years I have longed for a little girl like you,' said the old woman. 'I am sure we shall get on splendidly together.' She began to comb Gerda's hair, and as she combed so Gerda forgot about her home and little Kay, for the old woman was an enchantress. But she was not a wicked witch, and there was no evil in her magic. She worked spells only for her own amusement, and she wanted so much to keep little Gerda with her. When Gerda was not looking, she went out into the garden and touched all the roses with her crutch, and immediately they sank down into the black earth, no matter how exquisite their blooms. Not a trace was left of them, for the old woman feared that the sight of roses might remind Gerda of her own and make her think of Kay.

Then she took Gerda into the flower garden. How lovely, how colourful it was! Flowers of every season blossomed side by side in glorious profusion. Gerda danced for joy and played beneath the cherry trees until sunset. Then she was given a fine bed with red silk cushions filled with sweet-smelling violets, where she slept soundly and dreamt as sweetly as a princess on the eve of her wedding.

Next day she played in the sunshine amongst the flowers, and so it went on day after day. Soon Gerda knew every flower in the garden, but although there were so many different kinds she could not help feeling that there was one missing. One day her glance fell on the old woman's straw hat with the flowers painted round the brim, and the most beautiful of all was a rose! For the old woman had forgotten to remove it from her hat.

'What!' exclaimed Gerda. 'Are there no roses here?' And she ran all over the garden, searching and searching, but not a rose could she find. She flung herself on the ground and sobbed her heart out, and her tears fell on the very spot where a rose-bush had sunk into the ground. As soon as her warm tears touched the earth the rose shot up as beautiful as ever, laden with blooms. Gerda threw her arms round it and kissed each bloom in turn, and she remembered her roses at home and her little friend Kay.

'How I have frittered away my time!' she exclaimed. 'I should have been searching for Kay! Do you know where he is?' she asked the roses. 'Is he dead?'

'He is not dead,' they replied. 'We have been under the ground for a long time, where all the dead dwell, and there was no sign of Kay.'

'Thank you,' said Gerda, and went to the other flowers, peeped into them and asked, 'Don't you know where little Kay is?'

All the flowers stood drinking in the golden sunshine and dreaming their own dreams, but none of them knew anything of Kay.

The fire lily told a story of India, but this was of no interest to Gerda. She turned to the pale blue wind-flower, and what story did he have to tell her?

'By following a narrow path, you come to an ancient castle. The old red walls are covered with thick creepers right up to the balcony, and there stands a beautiful girl. She leans over the balustrade, gazing down to the path. No rose upon its stem is as fair as she, no apple blossom is as gentle as she, as it is borne on the breeze that rustles her silken gown. Isn't he coming yet?'

'Do you mean Kay?' asked Gerda.

'I am telling my story, my dream,' replied the wind-flower.

And what did the snowdrop have to say?

'A swing hangs from a tree on long, long ropes, and two little girls are swinging on it, their snow-white dresses fluttering in the breeze, the long green ribbons streaming from their hats. Between them stands their little brother. In one hand he is holding a bowl of soapy water, and in the other he holds a clay pipe. He is blowing bubbles, lovely bright bubbles which hover in the air all around them. A new bubble is even now quivering on the pipe, eager to be set free. A little black dog hops on its hind legs, wanting to swing too. The swing goes up, the little dog falls and barks, the bubble bursts. That is my dream – a swing and a bursting bubble.'

What about the hyacinths?

'There are three beautiful sisters, fair and gentle. One of them is dressed in red, the second in blue and the third in white. Hand in hand they are dancing in silvery moonlight on the banks of a calm lake. They are real girls – not fairies. The air is filled with a sweet perfume which becomes stronger and stronger. The girls lie down in three coffins which are borne away over the still waters of the lake. Fireflies hover like tiny lights. Are the girls dead? The perfume of flowers seems to say that they are. The church bells are tolling.'

'You make me sad,' said Gerda. 'Why should the girls be dead? Is Kay dead? The roses have been under the ground and they assure me he is not there.'

'Kling, klang,' rang the hyacinth bells. 'We are not ringing for Kay. We do not know him. We are telling our own story – the only one we know.'

So Gerda went to the buttercup, whose bright yellow petals peeped through the long grass.

'You look just like a little sun shining there,' she said. 'Can you tell me where I can find my friend?'

The buttercup smiled sweetly at her. What sort of a story would it have to tell?

'I see God's golden sun shining into a little courtyard on a fine spring morning, lighting up the old stone walls and the cobbles. An old grandmother is sitting in a rocking-

chair, enjoying the sun's warm rays. The sun tiptoes lightly over the cobbles and kisses the old lady, and its kiss is golden – the pure gold of love and kindness and joy. Isn't that a good story?' said the buttercup.

'Oh, my poor old grandmother!' sighed Gerda. 'I am sure she must be worrying about me. But I shall soon be home, bringing Kay with me. What is the use of asking all these flowers for news of Kay when each of them knows only its own story?'

She tucked up her skirt in order to run faster, but a daffodil brushed against her knees as she was leaping over it, and whispered, 'Do you know what?' So Gerda bent down to listen, and this is what she heard.

'I can see me,' said the daffodil. 'I can see myself! Oh, how lovely I am! Up in the attic I see a dancer skipping about half dressed, now on one leg, now on the other. She seems to be treading the whole world under foot. Now she is pouring water out of a teapot on to her bodice. Cleanliness is a beautiful thing. Her little white dress is hanging on a peg. She takes it down and pours water on it from the

212

teapot, and hangs it up to dry. Now she is putting it on and is tying a saffron yellow scarf round her neck, making the dress look even whiter. Slowly she stretches one leg up, raising it high. See! She is like a flower on a stalk! I can see myself! I can see myself!'

'Why are you telling me all this?' asked Gerda impatiently. 'None of this concerns me.' And she hurried out of the garden.

The gate was locked, but the catch was almost eaten away by rust and broke as soon as she twisted it. Gerda took a quick look over her shoulder to see if she was being followed, and fled from the garden in her little bare feet. She ran and ran until she was out of breath, and then she sat down to rest on a boulder. As she looked about her she saw that summer had passed and it was now autumn, for all the seasons in the enchanted garden were mixed up together and she had no idea how long she had been there. 'How long I must have stayed!' she exclaimed. 'It is autumn already and I have no time to lose.' And she rose and hurried on her way.

The weather grew colder, and her little feet were sorely cut and bruised on the rough, stony ground. The long willow leaves turned yellow and fluttered down one by one. Only the sloe still bore fruit. The whole world seemed grey and desolate.

Fourth Story

PRINCE AND PRINCESS

Weary and footsore, Gerda had to rest again. A great black crow came hopping through the snow and paused to observe her, cocking his head inquisitively from side to side and peering at her out of the corner of his eye.

213

'Caw! Caw! Good morning to you!' said the crow. He sat and watched her for a few minutes, and then asked her why she had come out all alone into the great wide world. So Gerda told her story and asked the crow if he had seen Kay.

'Possibly,' replied the crow, 'possibly.'

'What do you mean?' cried Gerda, and she seized the crow and almost squeezed him to death in her excitement. 'Have you really seen him?'

'Gently, gently!' protested the crow. 'I am not sure if it is Kay or not, but if it is he has certainly forsaken you for his princess.'

'Oh! Is he living with a princess?'

'Wait a bit, wait a bit!' said the crow. 'I find your language so intolerably difficult! Do you not understand crows' language?'

'I'm afraid I have never learnt it,' replied Gerda.

'Never mind,' said the crow. 'I shall have to explain to you as best I can.' And this is what he had to tell.

'In this kingdom there lives a princess who is extremely intelligent. It is said that she reads all the newspapers in the whole world. Shortly after she ascended the throne she began to wish she had someone to share her responsibilities, so she thought she would like to get married. This was a good idea, but she was determined to marry a man who could take part in good, intelligent conversation – a man who was interesting to talk to, rather than handsome and distinguished. So she called all her ladies-in-waiting together and announced her decision. "What a wonderful idea!" they exclaimed. "We should like to get married too." I assure you I am telling the truth,' said the crow. 'I have a lady-friend who is a tame crow in the palace and she tells me everything that goes on there.

'Advertisements began to appear in all the newspapers, to the effect that every good-looking young man would be

214

welcome at the palace, and that the princess proposed to select as her husband the young man whose conversation she found most entertaining. Well,' said the crow, 'I can assure you that young men hastened to the palace from all over the place – hundreds of them – but they all seemed to be struck dumb before the princess. No matter how brightly they chattered away in the streets, they seemed to lose the power of speech as soon as they came through the palace gates, past the sentries in their silver uniforms and past the gold-clad footmen on the great staircase. There they would stand, gaping stupidly up at the princess, with not a word to say for themselves. The odd thing was that they could talk well enough as soon as they came out of the palace again!

'What an extraordinary spectacle it was to see the hundreds of suitors queuing up along the royal avenue which led from the city gates to the palace! I went along to have a look at them, and a comical sight it was! Hundreds of them there were, all hungry and thirsty, for few of them had brought any food with them. Indeed, they had not expected such a long wait.'

'But what about Kay?' asked Gerda impatiently. 'Was he amongst them?'

'Patience, my dear, patience!' replied the crow. 'I am just coming to him. On the third day, when the crowd of suitors had faded away, a little fellow marched boldly up to the palace, with neither horse nor carriage. His eyes sparkled like yours and he had beautiful long hair, but he was poorly dressed.'

'That was Kay,' sighed Gerda. 'Oh, I have found him after all!' And she clapped her hands for joy.

'He carried a rucksack on his back,' said the crow.

'I think it must have been his sledge,' cried Gerda. 'He went away with his sledge.'

'Possibly,' replied the crow. 'I did not examine it very

closely. But my lady-friend tells me that he showed no sign of embarrassment as he strode past the silver-clad sentries and the golden-uniformed footmen. On the contrary, he nodded gaily to them and poked them in the ribs, saying, "How boring it must be to stand here all day long. I think I'll go in."

'The great halls were brilliantly lit. Ministers and servants went to and fro, bare-foot, carrying golden dishes, and the magnificence of the scene was enough to take your breath away. To crown all, the little fellow's shoes squeaked most dreadfully, but oddly enough he showed not the slightest trace of embarrassment.'

'It must have been Kay,' said Gerda. 'I know he had new shoes, for I heard them squeaking in Grandmother's room.'

'Oh yes, they squeaked,' said the crow. 'But he went straight up to the princess, who was sitting on a pearl as big as a spinning-wheel, surrounded by her ladies-in-waiting and their maids and maids' maids, and all her courtiers and their servants and the servants' servants, who in their turn had servants – and the nearer the door they stood, the more toffee-nosed they were. You would hardly dare to look at the servant's servant standing at the door in his long white stockings!'

'It must have been frightful,' said little Gerda. 'And did Kay win the princess?'

'Aha! My lady-friend told me all about it. He told the princess that he had not come to woo her, but to find out if she was really as clever as she thought! As it happened, they both liked each other immensely, and the princess was most impressed by his intelligence and ready wit.'

'Yes, Kay is clever,' said Gerda. 'He can even work out complicated sums in his head. Please,' she added, 'can you not smuggle me into the palace somehow?'

'That is more easily said than done,' said the crow. 'I

must have a word with my lady-friend about it, but, as far as I know, the regulations are strict, and you will never be able to enter the palace openly.'

'Surely it won't be as difficult as all that?' said Gerda. 'When Kay knows I am here he will come out and fetch me in himself.'

'Wait for me by the railing,' said the crow, as he ruffled his wing feathers and flew away.

He did not return till it was growing dark. 'Caw! Caw!' he said. 'My lady-friend sends you greetings, as well as this piece of bread which she filched from the kitchen for you. You must surely be hungry! It is no use, you cannot enter the castle. You don't even have shoes on, and neither the silver sentries nor the golden footmen would ever let you pass. But do not give up hope! My lady-friend knows of a little back staircase which leads directly to the royal chamber, and she thinks she can find the key.'

Gerda and the crow crossed the garden to the great avenue where the leaves were falling. When the lights in the palace had gone out, the crow led Gerda to the little back door, which they found ajar. How Gerda's heart beat with fear and joy! She felt very guilty, although all she wanted was to know whether Kay was alive and well. Surely he must be there! Already she could see his bright eyes and his long hair in her imagination, and saw him smile at her as he had done so long ago under the roses. Surely he would be glad to see her again and to have news of his home? How she trembled with fear and joy!

They had now reached the staircase. It was dimly lit by a lantern on top of a cupboard, and there stood the tame crow, glancing about her and looking Gerda up and down. Gerda curtsied, just as her grandmother had taught her.

'My dear,' said the tame crow, 'I have heard so much about you. I am only too delighted to be able to help you.

Take the lamp and follow me – we are unlikely to meet anyone this way.'

'I am sure we are being followed,' said Gerda a moment later. And, indeed, shadows swept past her on the wall – thin-legged horses with flowing manes, huntsmen, lords and ladies on horseback.

'Do not worry,' said the crow. 'They are only dreams.

They always haunt the palace at night. They will not harm you.'

They entered the first room. The walls were covered with rose-pink satin embroidered all over with flowers. They went from room to room, each more magnificent than the last, until they came to the royal bed-chamber, which was so beautiful that it almost took Gerda's breath away. The central pillar was like a golden palm-tree with graceful glass leaves that covered the ceiling. A pair of beautiful beds hung on either side, suspended from golden branches and shaped like lilies. One bed was white and in it lay the princess. The other was crimson, and Gerda supposed she would find Kay sleeping in it.

She stepped softly forward and pushed aside one of the red lily petals. She saw a sun-tanned neck. It must be Kay! She called his name aloud and held up the lamp – a cavalcade of dreams came galloping into the room. The young prince blinked his eyes and sat up – but it was not Kay! He looked like Kay only from behind, but he was still very handsome.

The princess now peeped out from her bed of lily petals and asked what was the matter. Little Gerda burst into tears and told the whole sad story between sobs, not omitting to tell how the crows had tried to help her.

'Poor child!' said the prince and princess, and they praised the crows for being so helpful and promised them a reward. 'Would you like to fly away free to the woods,' asked the princess, 'or would you rather stay here as royal crows, with full rights to everything that falls to the kitchen floor?'

Both crows bowed low and said they would like to stay on at court, for they were thinking of their old age and how pleasant it would be to have all their food provided without having to go and hunt for it.

The prince offered Gerda his crimson lily bed for the

night. He could have thought of nothing more fitting for her. 'How kind people are!' thought Gerda. 'How un-selfish!' With this pleasant thought she closed her eyes and slept. The dreams all returned with a mighty rush, and appeared to Gerda in the form of angels pulling a little sledge on which Kay sat and nodded to her, but when she awoke they had all disappeared.

Next morning Gerda was dressed from head to foot in silk and velvet. She was invited to stay at the palace for as long as she wished, but she asked her kind hosts for a little pony-trap with a pony to pull it, and a pair of boots so that she could continue on her way in search of Kay. She was given the boots and a muff, and as soon as she was ready, a golden coach came rolling up to the door, bearing the royal coat-of-arms. The coachman, the footman and the out-riders – for there were even outriders – all wore golden crowns. The prince and princess themselves helped her into the coach, and wished her a successful journey.

The crow from the woods, who had married his lady-friend in the meantime, accompanied Gerda for the first few miles. The other crow stood at the door and flapped her wings; she preferred to stay at the palace, for she had a headache as a result of over-eating since her appointment as royal crow.

'Farewell!' cried the prince and princess, and Gerda wept and the crow with her. They travelled the first few miles and then the crow too, bade her farewell. And this was the most painful leave-taking. The crow hopped on to a high branch and flapped his wings at her for as long as he could see the coach glinting in the bright sunshine.

Fifth Story

THE LITTLE ROBBER-GIRL

They drove on through the gloomy forest and the coach shone like a torch. This caught the eye of the robbers and drove them wild with greed.

'It is gold, pure gold!' they cried, and they fell on the coach, seized the horses by the bridles, killed the coachman, the footman and the outriders, and dragged little Gerda from the coach.

'Oh, she is plump and pretty!' exclaimed the horrid old robber-woman, who had a long shaggy beard, and eyebrows which hung down over her eyes. 'She has been well fed on nuts and other good food! She is just like a fat little lamb, ready for slaughter! What a tasty morsel she will be!' And the old woman drew from her belt a bright, shiny knife which flashed horribly in the sunlight.

'Ow,' shrieked the woman, at the very same moment. Her own little daughter, whom she was carrying on her back, had bitten her ear. 'You naughty child!' cried the mother. And so she had no time to kill Gerda.

'I want to play with her!' said the little robber-girl. 'I want her muff and her fine clothes, and she is to share my bed with me.' And she bit her mother again, this time in the other ear, so that the robber-woman leapt in the air and danced about in circles. All the other robbers laughed and called out, 'Just look at her dancing with her little girl!'

'I want to ride in the coach!' cried the robber-girl, and she was so vicious and self-willed that no one dared gainsay her.

She climbed in and made Gerda sit beside her. Off they clattered over roots and boulders, deeper and deeper into the wood. The robber-girl was the same age as Gerda, but stronger and broader in the shoulders, and her skin was

221

much darker. Her eyes were deep black and had an almost melancholy expression. 'They shall not kill you as long as I am with you.' She put her arms round Gerda's neck. 'Are you a real princess?'

'No,' replied Gerda, and she told her story and explained how she loved little Kay.

The robber-girl peered earnestly into Gerda's eyes, nodded, dried Gerda's tears and tucked both hands into her muff, which was beautifully warm.

Suddenly the coach came to a halt in the courtyard of the robbers' castle. The walls of the castle were crumbling, and ravens and crows flew in and out of the gaping holes. Enormous dogs, which looked big enough to swallow a man at one gulp, leapt up at the coach, baring their teeth, but not a sound came from their throats, for they had been trained not to bark.

A huge fire was burning on the stone flags of the old hall, whose walls and ceiling were blackened with smoke. There was no chimney and the smoke drifted round the hall till it found a crack through which it could escape. A great pot of soup was suspended over the flames, and hares and rabbits were roasting on spits.

'This evening you are to sleep with me and my animals,' announced the robber-girl.

They ate and drank together and then retired to a corner, where a pile of straw and rough blankets lay. On the rafters above them perched well over a hundred doves, which seemed to be asleep, though many of them stirred as the girls approached.

'They are all mine,' declared the robber-girl. She seized the nearest dove and held it upside down by the legs, letting it flap and struggle. 'Kiss it!' And she held it up to Gerda's face. 'The wood pigeons stay up there,' she added, pointing to a barred hole in the wall. 'They would fly away if I did not keep them well shut up. And here is Bo, my

222

special pet.' She dragged forward a reindeer by its antlers, and Gerda saw that the poor beast was fettered and had a heavy copper ring round its neck. 'I tickle his throat with my sharp hunting-knife every evening, just to make sure he is afraid of me.'

With these words the girl drew a long knife from a crack in the wall and ran its point across the reindeer's throat. The poor beast kicked and bucked, and the robber-girl laughed and pulled Gerda over to her bed.

'Do you take your knife to bed with you?' asked Gerda, looking at the girl fearfully.

'Oh yes. You never know what might happen. But tell me all about Kay, and about your adventures.'

So Gerda told her story. From the hole in the wall high above them came the incessant cooing of pigeons, which soon lulled the little robber-girl to sleep, with one arm round Gerda's neck and the other tightly clasping her knife.

Not a wink of sleep came to Gerda, for she was much too frightened. The robbers squatted round the great fire, eating and drinking, while the old robber-woman turned somersaults on the floor. It was dreadful!

'Coo, coo,' said the wood pigeons. 'We have seen little Kay. A white hen was drawing his sledge, but he was sitting with the Snow Queen in her sleigh. She drove through our wood when we were tiny chicks in the nest. Her breath was so cold that all the young pigeons froze to death – we two were the only survivors. Coo, coo!'

'Where was the Snow Queen going?' cried Gerda. 'Can't you tell me any more?'

'She must have been going to Lapland, where there's nothing but snow and ice. Ask the reindeer – he is sure to know.'

'Oh yes,' said the reindeer, 'Lapland is a fine country, plenty of beautiful snow and ice. There you can roam about through the broad, gleaming valleys! That is where the Snow Queen has her summer tent. Her castle is much further on towards the North Pole.'

'Oh, Kay, dear Kay!' sobbed Gerda.

'Lie still,' said the robber-girl, 'or you'll get my knife in your belly!'

Next morning Gerda repeated what the wood pigeons had said, and the robber-girl looked serious for a moment. Then, turning to the reindeer, she asked, 'Do you know where Lapland is?'

'I ought to know Lapland,' he replied, with an eager gleam in his eyes. 'I was born and bred there, and all my childhood days were spent romping about on the snowfields.'

'All right,' said the robber-girl. 'As you see, most of our men are away at present. Only Mother is there, and she has been drinking from the big flask and she is sure to doze off soon. The moment she is asleep I will do something to help you.'

She leapt out of bed and flung her arms round her mother's neck, tweaked her beard, and said, 'Good morning, my dear, sweet old goat!' And her mother gave her a cuff that made her nose black and blue. But it was all in play.

As soon as her mother had taken another drink from the bottle and drowsed off to sleep, the robber-girl took her sharp knife and went up to the reindeer. 'I should dearly like to keep you here, so that I could amuse myself by tickling your throat with this big knife. But instead, I am going to cut your rope and send you off to Lapland. How does that suit you? But you must work for your freedom. I want you to take this little girl to the Snow Queen's castle and help her to find her friend. I know you were listening when she told her story, so you know what to do.'

The reindeer leapt for joy and would hardly stand still for long enough to allow Gerda to climb on to his back. The robber-girl tied her on to make her more secure and even gave her a cushion to sit on.

'Here are your fur boots,' she said. 'You will need them in all that cold. But I keep your muff – it is so soft. But, never mind, you won't freeze! Here are Mother's long gloves.'

Gerda wept for joy.

'What's the matter?' asked the robber-girl. 'Aren't you pleased? Here are two loaves and a piece of ham so that you don't starve.' And she tied them all to the reindeer's back. When she was sure that everything was safe, she opened the door and called away the great dogs which were crouching outside. Then she cut through the rope with her knife and said to the reindeer. 'Off you go now, but mind you look after the little girl!'

Gerda stretched out her hands in the huge gloves to the robber-girl and said goodbye.

Away they flew over mountain and valley, through great forests, across marshes and plains, but the reindeer hardly stopped to recover his breath. Around them wolves howled and ravens croaked, and fiery lights appeared in the sky.

'Those are my beloved old Northern Lights!' said the reindeer. 'See how the whole sky is aglow!'

On and on they ran, day and night. When the bread and ham were finished they reached Lapland.

Sixth Story

THE LAPP WOMAN AND THE FINNISH WOMAN

They came to a halt outside a wretched little hut. Its roof very nearly touched the ground, and the door was so low that Gerda had to crawl in on her hands and knees. There was no one in the hut except an old Lapp woman, who was busy cooking fish over an oil lamp. The reindeer told her Gerda's story, but not before he had told his own, which he considered of much greater importance. Poor Gerda was so numbed with the cold that she could not speak.

'You poor things!' exclaimed the woman. 'You have many miles yet to go before you reach Finland. That is where the Snow Queen lives and spends the long dark nights burning strange fireworks. I will write a few lines on a dried cod – for I have no paper – for you to give to an old Finnish woman. She will be much better able to help you than I am.'

When Gerda had warmed herself and had eaten and drunk, and the woman had written her note on a dried cod, she set off again with the reindeer. All night long the sky glowed with the beautiful blue Northern Lights. At last they came to Finland and knocked on the chimney of the Finnish woman's house, for there was no door.

Inside the house it was so warm that the old woman wore almost no clothes. She was wizened and ugly, but hospitable. She helped Gerda off with all her warm clothes and her long gloves and boots, for otherwise she would have been far too hot, and laid a block of ice on the reindeer's head. Then she read the message that was written on the dried cod. Three times she read it, till she knew it off by heart; then she threw the cod into the pot to cook. There was little food to be had in this far northern land, so nothing must be wasted!

Once again the reindeer told his own story to begin with, then Gerda's, and the woman blinked her wise old eyes slowly, but said not a word.

'I know how clever you are,' said the reindeer. 'I know that you bind all the winds of the world with a single thread. If the sailor loosens the first knot, he gets a fair wind; if he unties the second, a strong wind; if he unties the third and fourth knots, there is such a gale that whole forests are uprooted. Can you give this little girl a potion that will give her the strength of twelve men, and enable her to overcome the Snow Queen?'

'The strength of twelve men . . .' mused the old woman. 'I wonder if that would help.' She went to a shelf and took down a large roll of dried animal skins. She unwrapped them and began to study, for they were covered with strange writing. So intent was her concentration that sweat began to pour from her brow.

Meantime Gerda sat in her corner with tears in her eyes, not knowing what she should do. Suddenly the old woman's eyes began to twinkle, and she drew the reindeer aside into the opposite corner. She laid a fresh block of ice on his head and whispered softly, 'Little Kay is in the Snow Queen's palace. He has everything he can possibly want and thinks it is the most wonderful place in the whole world. But that is due to the glass splinters in his eye and his heart. Until they are removed it is hard to see how he can remember his family and friends or, indeed, how he can think of anything but the Snow Queen and her palace. He is well and truly in her power.'

'But can you not give little Gerda something that will enable her to win Kay back from the Snow Queen?'

'I can give her no greater power than she already possesses. Can you not see how all creatures seem to serve her, and how she has come unharmed over such vast distances? Her power is greater than ours, for it lies in her generous and unselfish heart – the heart of a loving and innocent child. If she is unable to penetrate the Snow Queen's palace and free Kay from the glass splinters on her own, I am quite certain we cannot do it for her. The Snow Queen's estate begins two miles from here. Take her there and set her down beside the great bush with the red berries that is growing in the snow. Say not a word, but hasten back here without wasting a moment.'

And the Finnish woman lifted Gerda on to the reindeer's back, and off they went at a gallop.

'Oh, I have left my gloves and boots behind!' cried Gerda, as soon as she felt the biting cold. But the reindeer would not stop and sped on and on over snow and ice until they reached the bush with the red berries. There he set her down and kissed her on the mouth, and big tears trickled down his cheeks. Then he galloped away at great speed, soon vanishing into the white world.

There stood poor Gerda in the middle of icy-cold Finland without gloves and without boots. She began to run on as fast as she could. Suddenly a whole regiment of snowflakes advanced upon her, but these had not fallen from the sky, for it was clear and shone in the gleam of the Northern Lights. No, these snowflakes came straight towards her on the ground, and as they came they seemed to fuse and take on strange and terrible forms. Gerda remembered how beautiful the snowflakes at home had looked under the magnifying glass, but these were quite different – much bigger, and ugly and terrifying to look at. They were the Snow Queen's guards, and the shapes they took on as they formed and reformed were many and varied. There were some like hideous great hedgehogs, some like clusters of snakes with heads waving in all directions, and others like small fat bears with bristling fur. And they were all dazzling white – living snowflakes.

Little Gerda began to pray, and asked God for strength and courage. The cold was so intense that the breath came from her mouth like a column of smoke. And her breath became thicker and thicker and finally formed into little transparent angels, which grew bigger and bigger as they neared the ground. All had helmets on their heads and shields and spears ready in their hands. The bodyguard became more and more numerous until Gerda found herself surrounded by a whole army of angels. They advanced against the gigantic snowflakes of the Snow Queen, and shattered them into a thousand pieces with their spears. So Gerda walked on towards the Snow Queen's palace, and as she walked the angels stroked her bare hands and feet with their wings, sending warm blood pulsing through her veins once more.

But now we must see what Kay is doing. Is he thinking

of Gerda? Has he the faintest suspicion that she is standing outside at the castle gates?

Seventh Story

THE SNOW QUEEN'S PALACE

The palace walls were of driving snow, the doors and windows of biting winds. There were more than a hundred great halls, of which the biggest was many miles from side to side. All were brilliantly lit by strong Northern Lights. How vast, how empty, how icy and how glittering they were! No happy parties were ever seen within these walls, not even a ball for the polar bears so that they could dance to the music of the four winds; there was no one to play the fool there, not even a little coffee party for the white foxes as an excuse to gossip. And over it all shone the Northern Lights – beautiful and clear, but cold and hard, without a ray of life-giving warmth.

In the middle of the vast snow hall was a frozen lake. The ice was broken into thousands of pieces, but each piece was so like the others that they might all have been made from a pattern. And in the middle of this lake was the Snow Queen's throne where she sat when she was at home, secure in the knowledge of her own grandeur and magnificence.

Little Kay was blue with cold, but he felt nothing, for the Snow Queen had kissed away all his sense of cold and his heart was a lump of ice. To and fro he ran with the triangular fragments of ice, trying desperately to make something, as with a jigsaw puzzle. He had made a great many curious shapes which demanded considerable skill; for Kay was clever, and the glass fragment in his eye had, if anything, increased his intelligence. He even formed whole words, but one word he could never form, and that was 'Eternity'. The Snow Queen had said to him, 'If you can make this word, I will make you master of the whole world, and give you a new pair of skates as well.' But she knew he could not do it.

'Now I will fly to the warm south,' said the Snow Queen. 'I must have a look at the black craters of Mount Etna and Vesuvius and sprinkle a little snow round the edges. It is good for the vineyards and orange groves below.'

And away she flew, leaving Kay alone in the vast hall of ice.

He gazed at the ice fragments and thought and thought, concentrating so hard that his frozen heart cracked. Stiff and motionless he sat, looking as ice-bound as the great white hall around him.

At this moment Gerda came in through the palace gates. A bitter gust of wind almost blew her back again, but she prayed and the wind died down as if by magic. She advanced through room after room, till she came to the great hall with the frozen lake.

As soon as she saw Kay she flew to him and flung her arms about his neck, crying, 'My dearest Kay, I have found you at last!'

But not a sound came from his lips. He sat motionless, cold and stiff. Gerda began to sob, and her warm tears fell on Kay's chest, penetrated right into his heart, and the lump of ice began to melt. Kay looked at her with a puzzled expression in his eyes, and Gerda felt hope stir within her. A sad, sweet smile filled her tearful eyes as she sang him the song which they used to sing so long ago as they sat together under the roses in the window garden.

The result was unexpected, for it was now Kay's turn to burst into tears, and they flowed so freely that they washed the glass splinter from his eye. He recognized

Gerda immediately and exclaimed with joy, 'My dear little Gerda, what has been wrong with me all this time? Have I been ill? How cold it is here!' And he looked about him. 'How lonely and empty!'

He flung his arms round Gerda's neck, and she hardly knew whether to laugh or cry. They were both so perfectly happy that even the ice fragments danced for joy, and when they were tired of dancing they sank down of their own accord to form the word 'Eternity', which the Snow Queen had required of Kay before he could regain his liberty and become his own lord and master.

Gerda kissed Kay's cheeks and they began to glow with rosy health; she kissed his eyes and they began to sparkle like her own; she kissed his hands and feet, and the life returned to them. No matter now when the Snow Queen chose to return – the magic word lay there at his feet in glinting icy letters.

They held hands and walked out through the palace door, and wherever they went the wind died down and the sun came out. When they reached the bush with the red berries they found the reindeer waiting for them with a young female reindeer, whose udders were full of fresh warm milk, which she gladly gave to refresh the children. Then they rode without delay to the old Finnish woman's hut, where they warmed themselves beside the stove before setting out for the Lapp woman's hut. They found that she had been busy sewing warm clothes for them, and had even made ready a sledge.

Kay and Gerda now said goodbye sadly to their reindeer friend and to the Lapp woman. The first young birds began to twitter and the forest was full of green buds.

Suddenly they heard the pounding of hooves, and a superb horse appeared. Gerda knew it at once – it was one of the horses which had been harnessed to her golden coach. On its back rode the little robber-girl, with a red cap on her head and a pair of pistols tucked into her belt. She had grown tired of life with the robbers and was going into the wide world to see what was to be seen and what adventures were to be found. How glad they were to see each other again!

'A fine young fellow you are!' said the robber-girl to Kay. 'I cannot think why Gerda bothered to scour the world for you.'

But Gerda stroked Kay's cheek and asked for news of the prince and princess.

'They have gone to foreign lands,' replied the girl.

'And the crow?' asked Gerda.

'Dead,' was the reply. 'I am afraid the tame crow is a widow now and hops about with a black ribbon round her leg. She makes a great show of mourning, but she is not really unhappy. But tell me about yourself. I want to know all that happened to you and how you found your friend.'

So Gerda and Kay told the whole story, and when it was time to part the robber-girl promised to visit them in town some day. For the present, however, she was determined to seek more exciting adventures, so off she rode while Kay and Gerda continued on their way, hand in hand.

Wherever they went they found spring flowers peeping through the grass and the buds on the trees bursting into leaf. They heard church bells ringing, and recognized the houses and tall spires of their own city. They ran through the city gates to Grandmother's house and hurried up the stairs and into the attic room, where they found everything exactly as they had left it. Not a thing had changed. The clock ticked softly and the hands turned. But as they stood in the doorway it suddenly dawned on them that they had grown up.

The roses in the roof garden nodded in at the window and, outside, the little chairs still stood in their shade. Hand in hand Kay and Gerda sat down in the sunshine.

The cold, empty magnificence of the Snow Queen lay safely behind them like a bad dream. Grandmother sat in the sun by the window and read aloud from the Bible. 'Unless you become as little children, you cannot enter the Kingdom of God.'

Kay and Gerda gazed into each other's eyes, squeezed each other's hands and smiled. There they sat, grown-up, yet children, children at heart, and it was summer, warm, glorious, blessed summer.

Also in Young Puffin

STICK TO IT, CHARLIE
Joy Allen

In these two 'Charlie' adventures, Charlie meets a new
friend and finds a new interest – playing the piano. The new
friend proves his worth when Charlie and the gang find
themselves in a tight spot. As for the piano – well, even
football comes second place!

THE LITTLE EXPLORER
Margaret Joy

The little explorer is setting out on a long voyage. He is
going in search of the pinkafrillia, the rarest flower in the
world. Together with Knots the sailor, and Peckish the
parrot, Stanley journeys through the jungles of Allegria –
and what adventures they have!

THE SCHOOL POOL GANG
Geraldine Kaye

Billy is the head of the Back Lane Gang and he's always
coming up with good ideas. So when money is needed for a
new school pool, his first idea is to change the gang's name.
His next idea – to raise money by giving donkey rides –
leads to all sorts of unexpected and exciting happenings!

THE RAILWAY CAT AND THE HORSE
Phyllis Arkle

Alfie and his friends are very curious to learn that a valuable horse is going to be delivered to their station. Could it be a racehorse, they wonder? They soon find out that it's no ordinary horse, but one that's going to need very special treatment!

THE HODGEHEG
Dick King-Smith

The story of Max, the hedgehog who becomes a hodgeheg, who becomes a hero. The hedgehog family of Number 5A are a happy bunch but they dream of reaching the Park across the road. Unfortunately, a very busy road lies between them and their goal and no one has found a way to cross it in safety. No one, that is, until the determined young Max decides to solve the problem once and for all . . .

FAT PUSS ON WHEELS
Harriet Castor

Fat Puss, the roly-poly cat, is up to his old tricks, and has no end of adventures with his friends the Mouse family and Humphrey Beaver. He goes flying, is the hero of the football match and roller-skates into the river!

MR MAJEIKA AND
THE HAUNTED HOTEL

Humphrey Carpenter

Class Three of St Barty's are off on an outing to Hadrian's Wall with their teacher Mr Majeika (who also happens to be a magician).

Stranded in the fog when the tyres of their coach are mysteriously punctured, they take refuge in a nearby hotel called The Green Banana. Soon some very spooky things start to happen. Strange lights, ghostly sounds and vanishing people . . .

NO PRIZE OR PRESENTS FOR SAM

Thelma Lambert

Sam just has to find a pet to enter in the Most Unusual Pets Competition at the village fete, but the animal he chooses leads to some very unexpected publicity! When Sam decides he'll give his Aunty and Uncle a happy Christmas, the only problem is how can he earn some money?

These two entertaining stories about Sam's ingenuity and determination appear in one volume for the first time.

SUN AND RAIN

Ann Ruffell

It hasn't rained for seven weeks. The Smallwood family have had enough, and are sending off for all sorts of heatwave 'special offers'. First to arrive is Susan's rain-making kit, and soon a rain cloud appears in the spotless blue sky – one solitary cloud which is fixed firmly over the Smallwoods' house!